S0-BNC-280

Dear Reader,

I've always been fascinated by what makes a hero a hero. Especially in the context of the thrilling, dominating heroes who populate our favorite Harlequin Presents novels. For me, even the most irredeemable hero still has a core of something inside, a quality that just needs to be teased out by our spunky heroine.

Just like in *The Frog Prince*. I believe that depending on whichever version of the original Brothers Grimm tale you like, it took the heroine to not only see something heroic about the hero but also to give him that kiss or nudge or sometimes even to break the walls down—as in the case of Alessandra Giovanni, who makes Vincenzo see that at the core of him, he is a hero.

Especially when it comes to the woman he loves.

I hope you enjoy my version of *The Frog Prince*.

Tara

Once Upon a Temptation

Will they live passionately ever after?

Once upon a time, in a land far, far away, there was a billionaire—or eight! Each billionaire had riches beyond your wildest imagination. Still, they were each missing something: love. But the path to true love is never easy...even if you're one of the world's richest men!

Inspired by fairy tales like *Beauty and the Beast* and *Little Red Riding Hood*, the Once Upon a Temptation collection will take you on a passion-filled journey of ultimate escapism.

Fall in love with...

Cinderella's Royal Secret by Lynne Graham

Beauty and Her One-Night Baby by Dani Collins

Shy Queen in the Royal Spotlight
by Natalie Anderson

Claimed in the Italian's Castle by Caitlin Crews

Expecting His Billion-Dollar Scandal
by Cathy Williams

Taming the Big Bad Billionaire by Pippa Roscoe

The Flaw in His Marriage Plan by Tara Pammi

His Innocent's Passionate Awakening
by Melanie Milburne

Tara Pammi

THE FLAW IN HIS MARRIAGE PLAN

HARLEQUIN

PRESENTS

HARLEQUIN® PRESENTS®

Recycling programs
for this product may
not exist in your area.

ISBN-13: 978-1-335-89378-9

The Flaw in His Marriage Plan

Harlequin Enterprises ULC
22 Adelaide St. West, 40th Floor
Toronto, Ontario M5H 4E3, Canada
www.Harlequin.com

Printed in U.S.A.

Tara Pammi can't remember a moment when she wasn't lost in a book—especially a romance, which was much more exciting than a mathematics textbook at school. Years later, Tara's wild imagination and love for the written word revealed what she really wanted to do. Now she pairs alpha males who think they know everything with strong women who knock that theory and them off their feet!

Books by Tara Pammi

Harlequin Presents

Visit the Author Profile page
at Harlequin.com for more titles.

CHAPTER ONE

"LET'S GET MARRIED, PRINCESS."

Vincenzo Cavalli adopted his usual composed expression but it didn't come easily this time. Shock made it hard for him to pretend as if he'd been planning to say those words all along. As if they hadn't erupted out of some place inside him that he didn't even know existed.

Alessandra Giovanni—top supermodel and the most beautiful woman he'd ever met, froze in the act of pushing her hair back from her face, her expression arrested.

It was as if a circuit in his brain had shorted, bypassing years of unwritten rules he'd always lived by. Every step in his life for the last two decades had been planned meticulously, building toward a future he'd pictured for himself as a young boy denied everything—love and basic security.

Every step dictated by his final goal—to take over Brunetti Finance International and nothing else. Every hour of every day he'd poured sweat and blood into pulling himself up from poverty to be able to claim his birthright one day.

Pursuing Alessandra Giovanni had initially been a part of that carefully crafted plan, as he'd discovered Alessandra was attached to all the Brunettis, especially the matriarch of the family, Greta Brunetti, who had thrown his mother and him out to starve.

Asking her to marry him—no. That was as much a surprise to him as it was to her.

But now that the words were out, he found he meant them. And not because he was an honorable man who kept his word at all costs.

Honor had always been a luxury he couldn't afford—like shoes or three meals a day when he'd been growing up on the streets of Milan.

Honor had no place in his world.

No, this request was purely selfish. Maybe the first selfish, nonstrategic thing he'd done in a long time. In forever, actually.

It was irrational and illogical, but the shocked look in Alessandra's eyes, the quick flare of excitement she buried the next second, the flush of color dusting her cheeks as her chest rose and fell, the fast rush of blood in his own veins as he imagined facing the famed Brunettis with Alessandra at his side as his wife—he knew this was utterly right.

More than anything, he wanted Alex in his life. The chemistry of their instant connection had taken him aback when he'd hunted her down to this perfect corner of Bali. Their mutual attraction a useful tool he hadn't counted on. But now that he had her, he wasn't going to give her up.

As to the fact of her being connected to the very family he'd been planning to destroy for so long, he was certain he could persuade her to see his point of view. Once he explained his reasons, Alessandra would take his side. She wasn't a blood relative of theirs. She would understand his need to topple them all. Her strong sense of right and wrong, her championing of causes around the world—it was an innate part of her nature, a quality that only added an extra dimension to his already magnetic attraction to her.

He raised the glass of champagne in his hand while never breaking eye contact with her.

Clad in a sky blue bikini that hugged her firm breasts like a lover's caressing hands, she looked voluptuously beautiful. As a supermodel who had worked for most of the large international design houses, he hadn't been surprised by her punishing fitness routine. But the natural energy of the woman as she geared up to take on the world and its myriad injustices... It still amazed him.

The blue of the infinity pool they were standing next to, in the grounds of her private villa, with the backdrop of Bali's lush hills and valleys surrounding it, couldn't equal the breathtaking quality of Alessandra's beauty. Hers was not simply the beauty of flawless skin or perfectly symmetrical features or curves most women would die for, though she possessed all those things.

It was her imperfections that delighted him, the quirks that made Alessandra Giovanni one of the most beautiful women in the world.

The gap between her front teeth, that fresh-faced girl-next-door quality, the awkward, self-deprecating sense of humor, her mad obsession with the world of boxing, her incredible verve for life, the audacious drive to fix all the injustices of the world...

On paper, she'd been too good to be true, stoking Vincenzo's curiosity into a wildfire.

In real life, she was magnificent, a force to be reckoned with, and he'd stood no chance against her from the second their eyes had met.

And then there was her air of wary vulnerability that innumerable magazines and countless photoshoots had never managed to accurately capture.

It stared back at him now out of bright brown eyes. The quality that had kept him awake the past few nights. Even with her warmth wrapped around him like a vine.

She's innocent, the small part of his conscience that he hadn't been able to silence kept piping up. *She might be hurt.*

Not when he was making her a part of his life, he told himself. Not by offering her something he'd never even considered in his entire life. Not if he carefully explained his reasons, not with her innate sense of right and wrong.

"Married?" she repeated, her tongue swiping over that plump lower lip that millions of women over the world tried to emulate with collagen. Her eyes widened in her gamine face. "Don't mess around with me, V," she said, with a little laugh at the end. A rough, rasping sound that never failed to arouse him.

A brave little effort to hide her emotions while the madly fluttering pulse at her neck betrayed her. Using that moniker she'd allocated him that first day when they'd met as though it was a kind of shield against him. Against her own feelings.

This was what he liked about being with Alessandra—she was an open book, somehow having retained a genuine quality in a cutthroat world.

He finished his drink and dived headlong into the pool, his heart thundering loudly in his chest. When he reached her, he pulled himself out of the water, and stood, her body flush with his. Her warm breath feathered over his cheekbones.

He pushed a tendril of hair away from her temple, his fingers, as always, itching to touch her. Hold her. Possess her. "You should know by now that I don't say things I don't mean, Princess," he said, pressing his mouth to her cheekbone. He filled his hands with the dips and valleys of her waist, the hitch in her breathing as he touched her pinging over his nerves.

"Yeah?"

"*Si, cara mia.* The last few weeks have been…" He frowned, trying to locate the elusive word. He'd never lost himself in the sensuality of a woman as he'd done with her. He'd never lost his mind over a woman like this, period.

"Wonderful. Fantastic. Amazing," she added in a breathless tone, a stark honesty in her voice that he was coming to count on more and more.

He laughed, the sound of it strange to his own ears. "All that. And I find…" He pulled her closer until their breaths melded. Until her arms locked around his neck. Until she sank her long fingers into his hair and pulled his head down. Until their hearts beat against each other in a harmony of need and want. "I'm not ready to let you go, *cara*. I don't think I'd ever want to. So why not make it official?"

She let out a gasp. He could feel her trembling against him. "It's crazy. These entire last few weeks have been completely crazy."

"Crazy bad?" he added, a ball of something he didn't want to name lodged in his chest. He'd never waited on an answer with such gut-twisting anticipation. All his adulthood, he'd manipulated things into working his way. He'd taken, instead of asking. Because he'd learned early on that it was the only way he could have things. Now he disliked the feeling vehemently. Once he had her, he would never subject himself to it ever again, he promised himself.

"No," she answered promptly. "Crazy good. Crazy fairy-tale-esque, almost. When I'm with you, I almost feel like the princess you call me. I…"

He waited. On a knife's edge.

"But then I've never been bowled over quite like I've been by you. I was just about ready to give up on men, in fact. And the world, even. When I was younger, I heard this story of a girl rescued by a prince. And you…"

"I'm no prince, Alessandra."

She sighed and burrowed her face into the warmth of his shoulder. Her teeth sank into his skin at the juncture of his neck. And his body reacted instantly, pressing against her soft belly. "It's been magical. And no, I don't want it to end. I don't want to go back to real life." Big eyes held his, penetrating in their intensity. "Only we don't know everything about each other yet."

"Is it enough to know that until I met you I'd never ever considered sharing my life with a woman, ever? Is it enough to know that the last few weeks have truly taken my life in a new direction? Is it enough to know that the future you confided in me you want is the one I want too?"

She looked up and all the hopes and dreams of the world seemed to be shining from her eyes.

For an infinitesimal second, the intensity of that scared Vincenzo. Just for a second.

A wide smile turned her face into breathtaking beauty. "It is enough. Yes, V. Let's do this. Let's get hitched."

Any lingering doubts Vincenzo had about whether what he was doing was right or wrong got swallowed up by Alessandra's kiss. By the sweet taste of her lips, by the honest urgency of her desire as she pressed up against him, as she whispered she wanted him right then and there.

Vincenzo devoured her mouth, his hands reaching for her hips and buttocks. Within seconds, he'd pushed aside her bikini bottom and was inside of her, and that sense of belonging once again filled every inch of his limbs. A feeling of peace that he had never known enveloped him as she took his mouth in a sweet kiss.

And for a man who'd never shared his life with anyone, who'd already spent too many years on a certain strategic path, it felt like a benediction. An invitation to a future he hadn't known he could have.

The loud and persistent chirp-chirp of a cell phone somewhere woke Alex out of a dreamless sleep. She stretched her body and found the sweet soreness invade her limbs as a result of the passionate night before.

With a smile, she buried her face in the pillow next to hers. The empty pillow.

Of course, the man she'd married was a workaholic.

The sound came again. With a sigh, Alex got out of the bed and looked around. After several tries, she located the sleek cell phone in a drawer under a laptop.

And frowned. This wasn't V's usual cell phone.

The number on the screen amplified her confusion.

She knew that number. It was Massimo's.

Why was Massimo Brunetti calling Vincenzo? How would he even know him?

Ever since Greta Brunetti, the matriarch of the Brunetti dynasty, had welcomed Alex with open arms almost thirteen years ago as a teenager—after discovering her much-younger second husband had an illegitimate daughter from a previous fling—the Brunettis had become her adopted family, including Greta's grandsons, sired by the son from her first marriage. Despite being no blood relation to Alex, Leonardo and Massimo Brunetti had nevertheless embraced her, generously sharing their home and hearts with her.

But of course, Massimo was worried about her. They all were. Guilt assailed Alex as she thought of the last few weeks. She'd never planned to stay away from Milan for so long. She'd only meant to spend some time in Bali after her latest photoshoot getting her head on straight about her career, about where she wanted her life to go. She'd even turned her phone off, wanting a complete break from social media and endless phone calls.

Instead of focusing on her future, she'd met Vincenzo. And married him in secret.

And had postponed telling the Brunettis, because Massimo and Leo, and especially Greta, deserved better than to be told her momentous news in a voice message or via an impulsive text.

But now… Somehow, the technical genius that was Massimo had discovered that she was holed up with Vincenzo. How was that even possible? Why hadn't Vincenzo mentioned that he knew the Brunettis?

Alex finally hit Answer on the screen and scrunched her face. "Hey, Massimo."

"Alex, *cara*, is that you? What are you doing with Vincenzo Cavalli's phone?"

Alex bit her lip. Massimo sounded different. Something was wrong here. "Why are you calling his number, Massimo? How do you know him?"

A sense of urgency filled Massimo's voice. "Cara, listen to me. Vincenzo is…he's the one responsible for all the trouble we've been facing at Brunetti Finances. He's the one who launched the hacker attack on the cyber arm. He's the one who's been goading board members into getting rid of Leo. He's a…a very dangerous man, *bella*. He's been hitting us from all sides for almost a year now. Concerted attacks on all of us—me, Leo, Greta. He's even achieved ownership of Father's stock somehow."

All of us… Massimo, Leo, Greta.

And her? Was she some kind of target too?

Alex felt as if the ground was being stolen from under her. She sank to the bed, her knees shaking, her belly swooping in a series of never-ending somersaults. "Massimo, I don't understand. But why…how…"

"Leo's been trying to reach you for some time, *bella*, but you seem to have been incommunicado. We learned that this Cavalli was also in Bali, and we wanted to make sure you stayed clear of him. Finally, Natalie, who used to work for him, had the idea to call his old number to try and talk to him. We were running out of other options."

Alex was numb with shock and betrayal.

"*Cristo*, Alex! What are you doing with him? Why—?"

"I…if I organize a taxi out to the airport, can you get me out of here, Massimo?" Alex cut him off. God, she needed to get out of here. Now. Before Vincenzo came back. Before he charmed her again with his sweet words and addictive lovemaking.

"Of course. I'll… Alex, is everything okay?"

"Just…please, get me out of here. Now."

"Okay, *bella*. Just sit tight. Give me a few minutes to organize you a flight. Alex, whatever it is, Leo and I will fix it. We're here for you."

Alex ended the call before she started bawling on the phone. Before…

What had she done?

Why hadn't Vincenzo even mentioned the Brunettis? Why was he attacking them like this? There was no chance it could be a mistake. Massimo and Leo had been having troubles at the company for more than a year now. Even Alex had been peripherally aware of it.

And now the man she'd fallen for so hard, the man she'd married so quickly, far from being the romantic prince she'd thought him, was in truth the enemy.

But even hours later, as she flew home to Milan, without having even breathed a word to Vincenzo, Alex couldn't help wishing it was all a mistake.

That Vincenzo was not the man who had been wreaking destruction on her adopted family.

That he was not the man who remained a serious threat to Leonardo's CEO position on the BFI board.

That he was not the man who had been unerringly finding weak spots in one of the most powerful families in Milan and hitting them where it hurt the most.

CHAPTER TWO

VINCENZO STARED UP at the villa on the shores of Lake Como. The villa that had been the seat of the Brunettis' power for nearly two centuries.

He walked up the very marble steps where his mother had stood and begged Greta Brunetti to believe that her son, Vincenzo, was the old woman's grandson, sired by Silvio Brunetti.

Greta's own flesh and blood.

But two decades later, as he walked up the same steps again, there was no fear or doubt in him. Soon this would all be his. Power and confidence surged through him as he walked in through the huge archway into the lounge.

Of course, his sweet wife, Alessandra, had hastened his arrival by running away and hiding here. He didn't quite mind the acceleration in his plans though.

He enjoyed walking into the lounge to see them all assembled there—the matriarch, Greta Brunetti; her grandsons, Leonardo and Massimo Brunetti; their wives, Neha and Natalie, and, amidst them, sitting on the chaise longue, was Alessandra.

She looked up as he entered. And he found his pulse started racing, like a schoolboy's. Instead of the anger he had nurtured from the moment he'd returned to find her gone, he felt a pang of concern.

Her eyes were puffy and red rimmed. Light brown hair pulled into a messy bun that high-lighted the sharp cut of her cheekbones. A loose sleeveless T-shirt and denim shorts with pink flip-flops completed her ensemble.

No makeup touched the flawlessly boned face, no designer clothes showcased her stunning beauty, and yet she looked like a million dollars.

Hurt shimmered in those eyes as she held his gaze without blinking. As if she meant to look straight into his heart. As if she was trying to search for a speck of honor within him.

But she would fail. There was no honor in him. None at all.

He swept his gaze over her entire length and found a little satisfaction in spotting the diamond still shimmering brilliantly on her left hand.

Mine, she's mine, he wanted to growl like a savage beast.

"Running away without a word, *Princess*? This marriage thing is new to both of us, *si*, but we clearly need some ground rules," he mocked, refusing to acknowledge the two men standing there like sentinels, guarding her.

Leonardo Brunetti, CEO of Brunetti Finances Inc. A financial conglomerate that was synonymous with prestige in the rarified circles of Milan, the man he intended to replace. And Massimo Brunetti, the brilliant, technical mind behind the highly successful cyber arm of BFI—Brunetti Cyber Services—and the man that had captured his past associate Natalie's heart.

Men who had everything that should have also been his.

Men he intended to take everything from.

"You think there's any ground to stand on after what you've done, V?"

If she'd yelled it at him, he would've felt much more in control of the situation. But the shaken whisper… He didn't quite know to handle it, to stop it from disarming him. "Come, *cara*. Whatever questions you have, I'll answer them in privacy."

"You had numerous chances to do it in privacy. To explain what the hell you've been doing to my family. To at least…hint to me that you've been turning their lives upside down. You lost all those chances. You lost…" She bit her lip, her chest rising and falling. A wet sheen coating her eyes. "Just tell us…why."

"Why what?" he said through gritted teeth. *Maledizione*, he shouldn't have waited to explain it all to her when he so badly needed her to understand his point of view.

"Why've you been targeting them?" Frustration raised her voice. "Why did you arrange for Natalie to take down BCS before she fell in love with Massimo? Why did you use Neha's bullying stepfather to spy for you? Why did you buy up BFI stock until you could square off against Leo for the position of CEO?"

"I thought all those actions were quite self-explanatory," he said smoothly.

Alessandra stood up and took a step forward, breaking away from the group. The subtle scent of her hit him, bringing with it such vivid sensations of entwined damp limbs and sinful pleasure. Of long, warm nights and warmer sheets and soft gasps. Of intoxicating smiles that chased away the web of loneliness he hadn't even realized he'd woven around himself.

He saw the pulse at her neck flutter rapidly but when he raised his gaze to hers, the sheer depth of dismay in her eyes was a stinging slap to his senses. The same eyes that had looked at him with such affection and desire…

"You think this is all a joke?"

He tucked his hands in his pockets to stop himself from reaching for her. "It is not a joke, Alessandra, least of all to me. If it's still not clear, then let me make it so.

"I have spent most of my life working toward

this moment. Moving people and contracts and money like chess pieces just to arrive at this point.

"I intend to take over as the CEO of BFI. I intend to own the company outright. I intend to drive every Brunetti from the company until it's all mine. Only mine."

One lone tear drew a path over a sharply defined cheekbone. "Why?"

"I believe in taking what's mine. Especially when it's been denied me for so long. Especially…" He lost the fight against himself and reached out to catch the tear with his finger. Skin like silk beckoned a deeper touch, and he gave in to that too. Damn it, he'd never intended to hurt her.

He rubbed the line of her jaw with the pad of his thumb, marveling again at how much he wanted her to lean into his touch, how much he wanted her to take that last step and mold her glorious body against his. How much he wanted her to look at him as if he were her hero.

But he'd never aspired to be a hero in his life.

In fact, he was the furthest thing from being a hero. He didn't believe in self-sacrifice or putting someone else before him or in the happiness of others enriching his own.

No, he believed in taking, possessing, having. And keeping hold of what was his.

"Especially…when I've made a commitment

to having it in my life in the first place," he finished slowly, his voice gone all deep and rumbly.

A quick intake of breath. A parting of those luscious lips. A quick rush of color into her cheeks. She swallowed and looked up. And for an infinitesimal moment, he knew she was as lost in him as he was in her. In the magic they created together. In the indescribable, illogical thing between them that had made him take such a big step.

That made him stand here explaining himself to her even after she'd run away from him without a word.

"Alessandra?" Greta broke in, puncturing the magic.

Alessandra laid those doe eyes on him. "You think BFI should be yours?"

"*Si*. Since it was Silvio Brunetti that seduced my mother with a hundred lies, got her pregnant and then discarded her like yesterday's trash.

"Since my mother was called a whore, and she and I were accused of being beggars and liars and kicked out into the street by the woman you consider a stepmother. Since I was denied all of this privilege growing up, I decided that I wouldn't be satisfied with just a small part of it now.

"I want to see every last Brunetti walk out of this house, their heads hanging in shame.

"I am going to take it all."

"That's…" Her eyes wide in her face, Alessandra looked like he had sucker punched her. Her tall body swayed where she stood. When he took a swift step toward her, she jerked away, her beautiful face contorted in shock. "Greta would never do something like that. She welcomed me with open arms when I came here to live with my father, her second husband. She's more than a stepmother to me. She loved me even more than…"

Whatever defense Alessandra wanted to offer on behalf of Greta died on her lips as she turned to face the older woman. A soft gasp escaped her mouth, her body bowing as if against a sudden, forceful gale.

Truth shone in the older woman's eyes, the only remainder of an encounter she'd probably never given another thought to. Whereas it had become the foundation of his life.

The dirty accusations. The supposed higher ground of privilege. The utter lack of sympathy.

The entire room filled with a vibrating sense of shock, all heads turning toward Greta with various degrees of accusation. Except Alessandra. Even in the face of the older woman's guilt plainly written on her face, Alessandra still looked disbelieving. She looked as if she were the one dealt the hardest blow. Something he hadn't accounted for and should have.

Even the legendary Brunetti brothers looked horrified, their gazes alternating between their grandmother and Vincenzo in a parody that he would've laughed at any other time. A string of colorful curses spewed from Massimo's mouth while Leo stared in numbed silence.

"We could do a DNA test, if you want to lend legitimacy to my taking over what should be mine," Vincenzo added dismissively. "I'd quite like to keep my mother's name though. There's a certain poetic justice in heading the prestigious BFI with her name, *si*?"

"We will take your word for it, Cavalli, though you're quite the spiteful bastard," Massimo said evenly.

"That's mighty grand of you since your father and grandmother denied my mother even that small decency," he couldn't help adding, the very thought of the blankness in his mother's eyes filling his throat with a corrosive taste he'd lived with for far too long.

"And me, V?" Alessandra said in a soft entreaty. "Where do I fit into this sordid tale?" For all it was asked in a tremulous voice, it reverberated around him as if it had been fired out of a gun.

His gut tightened, a cold, clammy feeling drenched his skin. A feeling he tried to battle and dominate into submission. He found he had no answer to give her right then.

At least, not one that wouldn't shatter the painful hope glimmering in her eyes.

Not one that he could articulate in so many words.

Not in front of all of them.

She nodded as if he'd given her a clear-cut answer. As if his silence didn't end up damning him after all. And then she fled.

Alex suppressed the tears that threatened with a deep breath and a big gulp of water. God, she'd cried enough over him in the last week.

She looked out of the French doors at the neatly maintained acreage around the villa. The greenhouse that Leo had had restored on the grounds. The ancient wine cellar that had been restructured and repurposed to serve as brilliant Massimo's state-of-the-art computer lab.

The pride and sense of history of this place was in their blood. It was their legacy. Their place in the world.

A place, and a sense of belonging, that Vincenzo had been cruelly denied. Along with his share of the legacy. She'd never forgotten the utter sense of inadequacy, the powerlessness when she'd discovered as a teenager that her mother's husband, Steve, the man she'd always thought was her father, actually wasn't—remembered the desperate need to belong somewhere, anywhere, completely.

She could imagine the pain and loss a little boy might feel being rejected by his family, the scars that would carry over to the man. But to destroy Leonardo and Massimo after all these years... She couldn't abide that. She couldn't.

"You have to stop running away from me, *cara mia*."

The deep, bass voice carried over to her on the soft breeze from the open doors, playing over her spine as if she were a set of piano keys and he the maestro.

She stayed with her face averted from him. Like a coward. No, a woman who knew her own weakness and was assembling her armor. But it was time to decide.

To look into the eyes of the man who'd seduced her so thoroughly that she'd lost all her hard-earned common sense and rushed straight to the altar with him.

"You left me no choice," she said. Even after she'd learned the truth, even on the long flight from Bali, even the past couple of days until Vincenzo caught up with her, there had been a small part of her that hoped that they'd all gotten it wrong. That the man she'd fallen for and married in secret wasn't the same man ruining the very people she loved.

"If I'd stayed in Bali, you'd have gotten the boxing match you've been asking for and I'd have beaten you to a pulp the way my mind's working right now."

His laughter enveloped her. Her spine stiffened, but she was no match for the frissons that husky sound created in her. Or the scent of him that twisted like a screw in her lower belly. Or the memory of the warmth of that tight body covering her like a favorite blanket.

The explosive chemistry between them had been instantaneous, all-consuming, mutual. And apparently, had no intention of abating even when her heart felt bruised inside her chest and her brain rebelled.

"Then maybe I'd have deserved it."

"You think it's that simple?" she said, turning around, frustration driving the words out of her. "That I yell at you, or scream at you, or pound that gorgeous face into mush and then we're even?"

Their eyes met across the room and held. That stillness she found fascinating about him descended again. He reminded her of a jungle cat—all restless energy and contained violence, preparing every single move for an attack.

A white shirt unbuttoned showed off the tanned V of his throat, with an enticing glimpse of curls at the bottom. Dark smudges under his eyes told their own tale—he was as much of a workaholic as her.

He looked a little rumpled after the long flight chasing her, coming after the fact that he'd been working straight for thirty-six hours when she'd left him. The gray of his eyes deepened—the only signal in all his stillness that betrayed him. That told her he'd been just as consumed by what was between them as she had.

Even now as she looked at him, there was no doubt what her foolish heart and her greedy body wanted.

More of what he'd made her feel. More of those warm, lazy nights. More of the man who'd promised her she'd never be alone again.

More of him.

She cleared her throat, ashamed of how little control she had around him. "Natalie spent a lot of hours—at the risk of increasing wrath from Greta and Leo and even Massimo—trying to convince me that you're not the utter monster your actions prove. That long ago, you were the only protector she'd known against a cruel world. That she owes you a lot. At a time when there was nothing she could do for you in return."

His gaze became opaque, but Alex noted the stiffness of his shoulders. "Didn't she tell you that I did demand a price for all that I've done for her, in the end?"

"You're surprised she stuck up for you. Are you that much of a villain then?"

"I don't know if I'm a villain, *Princess*. But I'm definitely not a hero," he said, walking into the expansive room and completely owning it in a matter of seconds.

Greta had gone to great pains when Alessandra had moved in to create a welcoming space for a lost teen. Every inch of this room had been a haven to a girl whose own mother had broken her heart repeatedly.

"I thought Massimo had all the rights to Natalie's loyalty," he said so softly that she could barely make out the words.

"I'm sure they wish it was that simple, that one emotion for one person could trump or cancel out the emotion you feel for another. But it doesn't work like that, does it?"

His head jerked. She'd chinked that armor, she was sure.

But when he spoke, his voice was as cool as ever. "I will admit I do not have much experience with emotions and family and all the complex, twisted drama that comes with it, *si*? So, no, I've no idea how it works.

"But if Natalie's misguided loyalty toward me—she was a fierce little thing even as a teen—paints me in a different light in your eyes, then I will thank her for it.

"Don't look for redeeming qualities in me that don't exist, *cara*. Don't forget either that I'm the same man you married recently."

The sheer arrogance of his statement swept through Alex like a wave threatening to drag her under. "You expect me to just shove everything you've done to them under the rug and carry on with you as though nothing has happened?"

"What if you learned that I had done all this—" his arms swept out to encompass the villa "—*to them*, for no other reason than that I was a cutthroat businessman who wanted to rule the finance center of Milan and BFI is automatically the first target?"

Afternoon sunlight gilded his face, caressing it with loving hands.

Her breath hitched in her lungs as she suddenly saw the resemblances she'd never seen before. The set of his eyes—so much like Massimo's, especially when he was smiling. The curling disdain Vincenzo's mouth so artfully expressed—exactly like Leo's when he was displeased.

So many small things hit her, causing her heart to stutter. Ramming her conscience again and again with the fact that he belonged here, in this place she'd called home. Weakening her anger. Confusing her hurt with too many emotions he far too easily evoked.

"That you can even think it could ever be that simple…shows how completely differently we're wired."

"Fine. How about we forget the whole cursed lot of them for a few minutes?" A little frustration slipped into his voice.

"You're the one who entangled me in this."

"Our marriage can stand outside of all this Brunetti drama, Alessandra."

"That's where you lose me, V. Maybe that's

what comes of playing with people's lives like you're conducting a chess game. Maybe you're incapable of seeing that to demand my loyalty while at the same time you're destroying them… is impossible. I can't see how we can possibly go forward from here… *Because you lied to me.*"

"Not a single time did I lie."

"Fine. If you want to split hairs, then you hid a great big truth from me.

"I'm *trying* to understand what you might have felt as that little boy, why you chose this path of revenge years ago. How much Greta's momentary thoughtlessness might have hurt—"

"I wouldn't refer to calling my mother a whore and a gold digger as a momentary thoughtlessness," he said, baring his teeth in a growl. "I grew up destitute, thanks to her. My mother had a mental breakdown she never recovered from. She lost her livelihood, and we were turned out onto the streets. It turned into early onset dementia."

Her heart thumped in her chest, the anguish in his eyes dissolving her righteous fury. Still, she had to try. "That *is not* Greta's fault."

"No? That my mother went untreated for so long, that she had a mental breakdown and that she didn't even have access to the minimum level of medical care is their fault. That she now lives needing round-the-clock nursing care is their fault." He reminded her of a wild animal, hurt and pouncing to attack. "That her disease spread so far and so fast that she doesn't even recognize me is totally their fault."

"She doesn't recognize you?" Alex whispered, her heart breaking for him. For herself too.

Because how was she to cross this divide caused by him holding on to his pain and fury for so long? How could she hope to turn him from this path of destruction when he was utterly determined to see Leo and Massimo as enemies, when his hatred had such strong foundations in his terrible childhood.

And if she stayed with him, knowing his plans for people she loved so deeply, what did that make her?

He shook his head, his jaw tight. "She thinks I'm still a ten-year-old boy. She's…frozen in that year."

"Why didn't you tell me any of this?"

"Because I don't want the pity I see in your eyes."

"Then what do you want from me?"

As she watched, half fascinated, half furious, he reined all that emotion back in. As easily as if he'd packed it away and locked it up. No, instead he channeled all that pain into hatred, into fury, into revenge. "The vows you made to me. The future we promised each other. That's what I want."

"I still can't believe Greta could've done something so—"

"Because you're buried under the weight of your obligations to them. You don't know their true colors—you're not tainted by the privilege and power that resides in their blood."

"And you think that means I can't love them just as much? When I found out Carlos was my biological father and came to live with him, Greta was already married to him and didn't even know I existed. But she welcomed me with open arms, she made a home for me here, she was the rock in my life when he died. Leo and Massimo, they accepted me and treated me like a real member of their family. You can't imagine what they mean to me, Vincenzo."

"And yet you presume to understand my animosity toward them?"

The leap of anger in his eyes—so unusual, especially directed at her—gave Alex pause. She wanted to try and see this from his point of view, but he'd put her smack-dab in the middle of it.

She took a deep breath and chose her words carefully. "You're right. It's nothing but lip service of me to say that I...understand what you went through. But you...you don't know what life was like for Leo and Massimo with your father, Silvio. They're innocent of any wrongdoing. They don't deserve to have their lives ripped apart like this.

"Your true culprit is Silvio Brunetti. Not them. But he's dead now."

He shrugged and the casual cruelty with which he did it with no pause to even consider her entreaty felt like a slap. "They bear the name I've hated all my life. Anyway, there are always casualties in war, *cara*. It's unavoidable."

Her heart sank. "Is that what this is, V? War?"

"*Si*. One I have waged for a long time. One I've invested everything into. I looked for weaknesses, sore spots, for years. I hit them with everything I had. And I don't intend—"

"Wait…" interrupted Alex, a cold finger raking its way down her spine. Pieces falling into place emerging in a picture that made her want to run away again.

Alessandra Giovanni: Supermodel. Style Icon. Businesswoman. Philanthropist. Adopted Daughter of the Powerful Brunettis of Milan.

She remembered the headline now.

That feature had been released in a magazine no more than a few days before she'd flown to Bali for yet another photoshoot.

Where the mysterious, gorgeous, gray-eyed Italian businessman had showed up.

Their accidental meeting when she'd visited the ruins of an old temple…

Their shared love of ancient architecture…

The three hours he'd waited the next day while

she finished her shoot, as if there was no other place on earth he'd rather be, those gorgeous eyes eating her alive.

The promise to show her sights she'd never see on a formal touristy visit...

Their first kiss under the most magnificent waterfall...

The questions about her charity, about the business she planned to launch, about all the things near and dear to her... The way he'd left her wanting more after that first night of intimacy on the balcony of her villa... The fairy-tale proposal and the marriage vows he'd recited in that deep voice...

Had any of it been real?

Nausea threatened to flood her mouth. "Did you come to Bali specifically looking for me? To see if you could use me in this *war* of yours?"

He didn't precisely flinch but she knew him. Knew every small shift and jerk of his beautiful face.

"Answer me, Vincenzo," she screamed, the question bursting out of her on a wave of fury and unspeakable hurt.

"*Si.* I did come looking for you. Alessandra—"

"Because that article quoted Greta as saying, 'Alessandra is the one I love the most in the world,' right?"

Again that dreadful, soul-crushing silence.

Despite her best efforts, tears broke out onto

her cheeks, making her vision fuzzy. Distorting those clear-cut features. Twisting that sensuous mouth.

"I looked for weaknesses, sore spots. I hit them with everything I had."

It hadn't been enough that he'd come after BFI and BCS. Or that he'd somehow achieved ownership of Silvio Brunetti's shares in BFI. He'd had to hit them where it would hurt them personally too, hadn't he, especially Greta?

Everything had been premeditated. Planned. Perfectly executed.

And she'd fallen for him like a ton of bricks.

She turned and faced him, wiping her cheeks roughly. Hurt gave way to anger, to a fury unlike any she'd ever known. "So how do you see this whole thing playing out exactly? What is it that you expect of me while you wreak havoc through these people's lives? People I love, let me clarify."

"I expect you to do what you'd have done if you hadn't found out. To give our marriage a real chance. To spend the rest of your life with me. To keep the vows you made to me."

"Our marriage is nothing but a…farce."

"No! I married you, Alessandra. I promised to spend the rest of my life with you. It is not something I undertook lightly."

Alex searched his face, hoping to see a flicker of something that she could hang on to. That implacable gaze didn't soften. Slowly, his words sank in, bringing yet more questions.

"Why? Why did you marry me? Why not just seduce me and walk away? I made it so easy for you anyway. I begged you to take me to bed. I chased you for the entire week after you showed up in Bali. I…you could have just walked away after we slept together. You could have dumped me—told me I had been nothing but a toy to play with."

"I do not treat women like toys. That's a Brunetti specialty."

"Then why?"

"You're beautiful, you're smart, you're a treasure any man would love to possess. For a man who grew up with nothing, who would always remain a bastard, who built his empire by trampling all the people in his way, you're the real prize, Alessandra.

"I married you because for the first time in my life, I saw something I wanted outside of revenge and everything it stood for. Outside of a campaign that has consumed me for the last twenty-odd years.

"I married you because taking you for myself was the final icing on the cake. Because taking you from that old woman makes it all complete."

Alessandra nodded, her stomach falling. "I don't know what to say to a man who thinks he can take me from the woman who gave me a home, who thinks I'll support the total destruction of my family. Who thinks possessing me somehow…improves his standing in the world. I will not…"

God, she wasn't going to be used again in a battle between people she cared for.

She'd done that and had the scars to show for it.

She wasn't going to be anyone's weakness. Or anyone's weapon. "I'm not a prize. To be won. To be possessed. To be snatched from someone's hands. To be used as a weapon against someone else." Alex forced herself to meet his gaze. "I want you to leave. Leave this house. I can't deal with this now… Please, leave, V."

He stood there, unmoving, unaffected, like a bloody big boulder that not even a gale of wind could budge.

After what felt like an eternity, he nodded. And left.

Alex stood there at the window, her throat dry. Her chest empty.

Of course, he hadn't married her for herself.

She wasn't a princess and this wasn't a fairy tale where she could magically wave a wand or press a kiss to Vincenzo's mouth and her frog would transform into a prince.

"She's gone."

"What the hell does that mean?" Vincenzo

barked the question at the carelessly lounging figure of Massimo Brunetti.

He tucked his hands into his pockets and stared down at the two men relaxing in their chairs on the balcony on this unseasonably cold early June afternoon.

The drive up to the villa had been just as spectacular as it had been the first time around. He looked at it with the objective eye of a man who meant to cut it all up to pieces and scatter it into the wind.

But as much as he relished the idea of destroying the very symbol and stronghold of the Brunettis' centuries-long power and privilege, other concerns rode him harder right then.

Alessandra hadn't returned his calls in five days, forcing him to visit the ancestral home again.

His patience, always on thin ice these days, was spiraling into a monster of a temper after this latest stunt from his sweet wife.

Cristo, it had been the worst week of his professional and personal life.

Beginning with a huge crisis in the finance department of his company, followed by Alessandra jumping on a flight out of Bali to Milan without informing him. Then his own long flight to catch up to her, their ill-timed confrontation that had quickly spiraled out of control thanks to the Brunettis bringing her up-to-date with all his supposedly Machiavellian motivations, followed by an urgent call from the twenty-four nurses that looked after his mother demanding his immediate presence at his estate in Tuscany.

Which meant he'd been forced to leave Alessandra alone for too long, letting the doubts he'd seen in her eyes fester and harden. He had loathed giving her that time apart from him, especially when it was spent around the Brunettis, who were more than happy to fill her ears with poison against him.

But he'd had no choice but to go to his mother. Usually, he didn't mind dropping everything in his empire to look after her.

"You shouldn't have left her like that..." Leonardo offered in an almost polite voice, his expression thoughtful. "Not so soon after she found out your true colors. The least you could have done was let her rage at you, maybe even let her throw one of her powerful punches at you. Anything would have been better than to leave her alone to stew in your betrayal."

"I didn't betray her—" Vincenzo bit out and then calmed himself with a discipline that was hanging by its last thread.

He had not betrayed Alessandra. He had simply left out a chunk of truth that he'd hoped to explain in full later on. He'd hoped to appeal to her strong sense of justice and fair play. He'd totally miscalculated the depth of her attachment to this group of privileged, spoiled Brunettis. "I had obligations I had to meet. Now, how about you tell me where the hell she is?"

"We *don't know* where Alex is," Massimo said. "After you left, she locked herself in her room, and when Natalie went to check on her the next morning, she was gone."

"You expect me to believe Alessandra didn't ask you for help to hide from me? That you didn't happily join in this childish game to thwart me?"

"You're right," Leo added. Still no rancor in his voice. Only a mild curiosity. "We'd have happily joined in. You went after the one person who had nothing to do with all this. But you're forgetting that Alex has connections in high places, all over the world.

"There's no shortage of people that will happily help her out, to save her from an untenable situation.

"She's the most loyal person I know, even if the person getting it is questionable.

"Knowing how much you despise even our name, she'll twist herself around to not give you any more ammunition against us. She knew you'd demand to know where she is. Keeping it a secret is her way of protecting us."

"She fought with me like a lioness because she thinks she needs to protect you from me. And you didn't come to her aid?"

"You're not listening, Cavalli. Alex's long

gone. No one here knows when she'll return or even if she will."

For the first time in a week, Vincenzo felt the sure ground under his feet shift. There was no gratification in Massimo's voice or Leonardo's gaze crowing over the fact that Alex had trumped him. Only worry for her. "She can't escape from her life. She has obligations, a global career," he protested.

"A career she's been slowly decoupling herself from. If you knew her at all, you'd have known she's been finishing up all her contracted work and not signing up to anything new," Massimo said. "*Cristo*, you really did a number on her at an already rough time, when she's been questioning everything about herself, her career, her life."

"What are you talking about?" Leo asked his brother the question that Vincenzo wanted to.

"She broke it off with that photographer boyfriend of hers—Javier Diaz—a few months ago. She plans to quit modeling altogether. I've been wondering why she'd marry a practical stranger after—"

"Alessandra and I have known each other for a few weeks," Vincenzo put in. But he was slowly losing ground. Losing his belief in her.

Had her vows to him meant nothing at all? Damn it, why hadn't she fought with him? Demanded an explanation? Given him the chance to convince her his motives were sound?

"It still makes you a stranger. But now I think I see it." Massimo's gaze bored into him. "You were a rebound from Javier. An escape. A temporary madness."

Vincenzo was more than tempted to knock the smirk off the tech genius's face but it went against everything he believed in. "Watch your words, Massimo."

"Walk away, Cavalli." The younger man stood up. "It hasn't dawned on you yet, has it? Alex has gone. It's what she does when the pain gets too much for her."

Vincenzo had no retort. No words, even.

This wasn't the Alessandra he knew. The sophisticated and yet vulnerable minx that had demolished his self-control with one genuine smile. This was not the woman who'd seduced him by giving away pieces of herself. The woman that had distracted him from twenty years' worth of strategizing in a mere few weeks.

But then how much did he truly know Alessandra beyond the report a PI had provided him with, beyond the picture the media painted of her?

"I'm supposed to believe that this complicated woman…is the woman I married?"

"It doesn't matter whether you believe us or not. We've known Alex for a long time," Massimo pointed out, satisfaction pouring out of every word. "You betrayed her trust. Learning about how Greta treated you was a double betrayal for her to have to deal with. And if I know your convoluted, labyrinthine mind—and I'm beginning to—you had every intention of using her against us," he said with a shrewd gleam in his eyes that for Vincenzo was far too much like looking in the mirror. "And I'm guessing she knew that. But then Alessandra has always known her own weaknesses," he finished cryptically.

Vincenzo had had enough. "If this is her way of telling me to pick between her and my original intentions, then she—"

"If she'd thought she could convince you to abandon this crazy revenge you're bent upon—" Leonardo's dark gaze held the first stirrings of anger in it "—she wouldn't have left her own home in the middle of the night *without* telling even us, would she? Which means you did nothing to reassure her. Nothing to prove to her that she wasn't just another pawn in your game."

"My plans for the Brunettis have nothing to do with her."

"Then you truly do not understand what family means to Alex. What family means at all." Vincenzo looked away, despising even the hint of sympathy in Leo Brunetti's eyes. "Accept she's gone, Cavalli. And that she's not returning anytime soon."

Vincenzo tensed, reeling under the other man's

words, fury and frustration building inside him. A future he hadn't wanted but had gotten used to looking forward to for the last few weeks was slipping through his fingers.

Was this the depth of Alessandra's commitment? To run away at the first sign of difficulty? To abandon their marriage because things had got tougher than she'd like?

Massimo gave him a pitying look. "I bet you anything she's gone running back into Javier's arms. Can't really blame her, can we, when her prince actually turned out to be a frog. And for all your scheming steel trap of a mind, I bet she won't be found until she wants to be."

CHAPTER THREE

Nine weeks later

THERE WAS GOING to be the devil to pay.

The very devil.

Alessandra stood near the bank of elevators, her feet rooted to the ground, staring across the vast white marbled lobby to the dark oak door that should bear the warning "Beware all you who enter here" or some such.

Everything in her wanted to run away from this. From *him*. But she was done running.

Her reflections in the metallic shine of the elevators—all six of them—had her second-guessing her direct arrival here at BFI's towers in Milan's financial district straight from the airport after her long flight from San Francisco.

She felt grungy in clothes that she'd worn for the last forty-eight hours. Her eyes felt permanently gritty from all the different time zones her body had had to endure in the past fortnight. But the one upside to her disheveled appearance was that no one had recognized her on either side of the Atlantic.

The last thing she'd had, after the initial hearing with the family court in the States and the subsequent meetings with her lawyers, was any energy left to charter a private jet to bring her over to Italy. And seeing that she'd already annoyed her agent; her two assistants, and Greta and Leo; Massimo—though at least he had sympathized with her actions and warned her she was just postponing the final reckoning—Javier; and the man sitting behind the oak door in front of her, she hadn't felt she could reach out to any of them and ask for a favor.

God, it felt like she'd been traveling forever, jumping from one painful situation to another, never stopping and thinking, never standing still.

Because if she did, if she stood in one place for more than a moment and allowed herself to look inward she'd have to listen to her heart. Her pathetic, bruised, still-foolish heart.

She'd have to face the fact that her mother was gone and the last time Alex had seen her, she'd said hateful words to her, that all the memories she had now were stilted, sterile meetings of the last few years. She'd have to swallow the bitterness she'd nursed when she'd realized her mother loved her little half brother, Charlie, far more than she'd ever loved her.

She'd have to face the fact that she had let that

same, soul-sucking desperate need to be wanted, to be loved push her into a disastrous marriage with a man she didn't even truly know, that she'd given her heart to a man who didn't even understand what that meant.

The image of Charlie's small, scrunched-up face, determined to look strong in front of Alex as she'd said goodbye to him, rose in front of her eyes, and she pushed away all the fears that could shake her resolve to do the right thing for him. For all her estrangement with her mother, she had fallen in love with Charlie from the first moment she'd set eyes on him as a newborn baby seven years ago.

Whatever the nature of her complex relationship with her mother, whatever insecurities she'd felt for years, whatever bitterness she'd nursed after Charlie's birth, she had to put all that away now. This was not the time for guilt or grief or regrets.

This was the time to take action. To make sure Charlie wasn't lost in the shuffle of adults' mistakes like she'd been as a child.

She had to stop running. She had to be strong for that innocent boy. She had to face the one man she never wanted see again in her life.

In the nine weeks that she'd been hiding, the world had exploded with all kinds of speculation about the mysterious billionaire Vincenzo Cavalli, who headed up Cavalli Enterprises, a finance shark that had its fingers in myriad industrial sectors.

That he was battling with Leonardo Brunetti for the position of CEO of BFI, although they didn't know why.

That he was a mathematical genius who'd made his first billion on the stock market.

That he was ruthless when it came to his opposition.

All the things Alex had been blissfully unaware of when she'd said yes to his sudden proposal.

She still couldn't assimilate the man she'd known in Bali—tender, funny and kind—with the man who'd been raining hell on the Brunettis with not a hint of conscience. And now she had to beg him to cooperate with her after hiding from him for nine weeks.

No, she wasn't going to beg. She was going to demand that he do this for her. She couldn't show weakness in front of a man who didn't understand the meaning of family.

"Mrs. Cavalli?"

"Don't call me that," Alex snapped.

"I'm sorry. You look…quite unlike yourself," came the tentative response from one of the receptionists hovering behind the huge swathe of gleaming white marble designed to intimidate anyone who dared assume they could approach the mighty Vincenzo Cavalli.

But not her.

She squared her shoulders. "Yeah, it's me."

"Shall I get one of the Mr. Brunettis for you? They're both in the building," a different woman asked, her perceptive eyes taking in Alex's state.

"No, thanks." Leo and Massimo, as powerful as they were, couldn't help her now. Only the devil she'd tangled with would do. "I was told on the ground floor that Mr. Cavalli has taken over this floor. Is that right?"

"Yes, he has. He's already made many changes—"

"Is he in there now?" Alex interrupted.

"Yes."

"Okay. Thanks, Miriam," she added, looking down at the shiny plaque sitting in front of the woman. "I'll just… Don't announce me."

The woman nodded, sympathy shining in her eyes.

Alex looked away. The chance to get a quick, quiet divorce had come and gone. Now she needed this marriage to work. And, oh God, Vincenzo was going to love that, wasn't he?

But only temporarily, she promised herself.

Whatever deal she made with Vincenzo, it only needed to last for as long as she needed him. After that, she would walk away forever. From his charming words, his penetrating eyes and him. Far away from him. From her own naive heart and its foolish hopes.

* * *

Vincenzo wondered if going so long without regular sleep was making him hallucinate. If his sanity was truly hanging by its last thread. Alessandra's continued absence—with not even a leaked rumor in the last nine weeks about where she was—had stripped away any semblance of civility from his demeanor.

Even his own team—people who'd been with him for more than a decade—were giving him a wide berth for fear of having their heads bitten off. He hated admitting it, but the ease with which Alessandra had walked out on their far-too-brief marriage rankled like a festering sore.

And still, he wasn't ready to give up. The creak of his door had him barking out a command to be left undisturbed.

His words stuck in his throat as the tall, lithe form of his runaway wife stood inside his office, her back plastered to the door, her white-knuckle fingers clutching the strap of her cross-body bag, neatly delineating the globes of her high breasts in a way he was sure she didn't realize.

"Hello, Vincenzo," she said, and then he knew she was real.

That soft, lilting voice, with its strange mix of American and Italian accents—he'd know it in his sleep. He'd had it whispered in his ear while he'd moved inside her body, finding refuge in it at long last, after never knowing it. Refuge that had been denied him for more years than he cared to count. Peace that he hadn't been able to afford however many millions he had made.

And then, just like a very vivid dream that you never wanted to wake up from, that refuge, that sense of peace had been snatched away from him.

No, she had snatched it away. At the first sign of trouble, she'd run. Very possibly straight into her ex's arms.

His heart thudded in his chest as he took her in, his blood rushing through his veins with a ferocious hunger along with a burning resentment for how easily she evoked his desire. But something was different about her.

This Alessandra looked nothing like the woman who'd worn her hurt in her eyes when she'd learned who he was, nothing like the advocate who'd argued passionately about the children she championed all over the world, or like the beautiful princess he'd taken to his bed for a night and decided to make his wife the next morning.

One night and he'd been lost. Enslaved as simply as if she'd woven a spell around him.

This woman looked as if she was barely held together at the edges.

Her clothes had seen better days. At first glance, she could be mistaken for a poor grad student with no time or energy for anything beyond academics.

Her hair was a glorious mess, a light brown halo around her face, the edges falling to those high breasts. Her skin had always been golden, but now she was tanned, as though she'd spent the whole of the last nine weeks outdoors.

Frolicking under the sun with her ex, perhaps, the insanely jealous part of him piped up.

But it was her eyes that transformed the panorama of her perfectly symmetrical face. They held a fire Vincenzo had never seen before.

Instead of guilt or shame or any of the other emotions he'd imagined he might see when she returned, pure challenge shone in her eyes. Her mouth, lauded for its pillowy pout, was set into a firm line. Now that he was over his shock, he recognized the energy, the determination pouring out of her very stance.

She didn't want to be here. But she was resolved to a particular action.

"Welcome back, Princess," he said, pushing his chair back, but without making a move to get up. He wasn't entirely sure his legs would hold him. His throat felt hoarse, his heart pounding away at a rate that threatened to send it bursting out of his chest. She'd been gone for weeks without a word, leaving him in a special kind of hellish limbo.

"Had enough of traipsing around the world with your ex?" he said, baring his teeth in a mockery of a smile.

She startled but recovered fast. Pushing away from the door, she ventured a few steps in. "That's the most ridiculous thing I've ever heard. I was nowhere near Javier."

The hotter the anger that flared inside him, the more Vincenzo forced himself into stillness. He'd be damned if he showed his fragmented self-control in front of a woman who'd run out on him at the first sign of trouble. "No? Both he and you conveniently disappeared at the same time for over two months. It's a logical conclusion."

She snorted, her nose scrunching with distaste. "You think I'd run away from one deceitful, dishonest man to another?"

Beneath the resentment still burning within, Vincenzo heard the truth in her indignation. He ran a hand through his hair, wondering at how far his jealousy had taken his thoughts. How much Alessandra's abandonment of their marriage had affected him.

How much he wanted the loyalty she gave so freely to the Brunettis.

"And yet, when I finally tracked him down on the phone, your ex wouldn't deny that you weren't with him."

She sighed. "That's because Javier, just like you, is a devious bastard. If he thought it would torment you, he'd say anything. He isn't particularly happy with me at the moment, like the rest of the world."

Vincenzo heard the weariness in her tone but it did nothing to assuage his own jagged emotions. Nothing to tell him that he was any different from that damned ex of hers. Nothing that would remove Massimo's taunting claim that Vincenzo had only been a rebound fling for her. "But he knew where you were, *si*?"

"Yes," she admitted, her gaze searching his face. "He got me in touch with a friend of his, a stud farm owner in Brazil." Something shifted in her expression. "But he wasn't with me at any point."

"And while you were having this extended temper tantrum on a stud farm in Brazil, did you wonder about what it might look like to me? Nine weeks, Alessandra, you were gone for nine weeks with no word. Not even a bloody text."

"You knew I was safe within a week of me leaving. I told Massimo to inform you."

Vincenzo caught up to her in two long strides, frustration mounting. Almost as tall as him, Alessandra looked straight at him, chin lifting, shoulders squaring. Readying herself for a battle. *Dio mio*, where was that seductively sweet, uncomplicated woman that had beguiled him in Bali? "I'm your husband. Being informed secondhand, especially by that taunting creep Massimo, that you're quite safe in some hole that you've crawled into is not acceptable."

The slender set of her shoulders tightened.

"What did you want from me, V? A call telling you that I was questioning everything you said and did with me, that I couldn't even bear to look at myself in the mirror because I'd made such a fool of myself, or that the thought of being near you while you happily destroyed Massimo and Leo made me physically nauseous?

"I needed to get away. From you. From Greta. From all of it."

"And?"

"And what? What's with the interrogation? How can you not see that all the promises we made to each other mean nothing when the foundation itself is cracked?"

The last bit of his temper frayed and his voice pitched dangerously low. "And if it's broken, you simply walk away, instead of fixing it?"

Still, she didn't back down. "Not if it's completely shattered, like my trust in you."

Tears and hurt were preferable to this version of Alessandra that looked at him with stony defiance and distrust. "I guess Massimo is right.

"The Alessandra that's lauded in the papers, that captures millions of hearts with her take-charge attitude is a sham. The Alessandra that said she'd always dreamed of having a big family is a lie.

"The woman I married is in fact an impulsive brat who runs when things don't go her way.

"Whose promises means nothing.

"Who clearly thinks marriage is only fun and sex and romantic escapades. Who's so immature that she can't even stand and communicate with the man she'd promised to spend the rest of her life with."

CHAPTER FOUR

IMPULSIVE. IMMATURE.

Words she'd heard before. Words she'd buried deep. Her mother, Alyssa, had used them far too many times in the conversations they'd had over the years. When Alex refused to take any kind of step toward healing their relationship.

From Vincenzo, the accusations rang true and stung deep. But it was the flash of disappointment in his eyes before he buried it under a thick veil of resentment that she couldn't ignore. It didn't help that she was already feeling fragile after attending her mother's and stepfather's funerals.

She'd expected Vincenzo's anger, had been warned by Massimo of the cold burn of it getting worse with each passing day. She'd chalked it up to an arrogant, ruthless man not getting his own way, probably for the first time in his life.

Away from his commanding presence, awash in her own hurt, it had been easy to forget that he had certain expectations of her, that her learning of his true identity and actions toward the Brunettis made no difference to him, to how he felt about their marriage.

"Running away from problems only makes them worse, piccola." Her biological father's wise words when she'd begged to come and live with him after yet another fight with her mother. But in the end, Carlos had indulged her wish, and as a result, the ocean of distance between her and Alyssa had become permanent.

Had she done the same this time too? What did she owe a man who had trapped her in a web of lies?

And yet, he'd gained nothing so far by marrying her.

"I married you because for the first time in my life I saw something I wanted outside of revenge."

Heat flamed her cheeks, but she refused to look away as if she was in the wrong. "If I apologize for my actions, it won't be truthful," she finally offered. "You left me feeling like I had no other choice than to go."

"And now, *bella*?" He leaned against his massive desk, throwing those long legs out in front of him. Pulling her starved senses to the sheer masculinity of him. As though she were a magnet and he was her true north. "Have you found one? Is that why you've deigned to return?"

With him standing no more than two feet from her, Alex weakened and let herself drink him in.

Take in the magnificent presence of the man she'd allowed into her heart.

Power and arrogance shimmered around him, a second skin. An armor he was using to keep her out now. But he hadn't done it in Bali. He had let her in. He had been a different man. Or was that just her naive belief in a fairy tale that didn't exist?

And how had she not seen the similarities between him and Leo and Massimo? The cut of his features, the very way he held himself slightly separate from the crowd, the affection she'd heard in his voice when he'd spoken of his mother—he was so much like his half brothers. So much a Brunetti through and through.

But she knew instinctively he would hate that comparison. The confidence in his speech, the commanding power of his look—it had been hard-won for Vincenzo and would be so much harder to shed too.

Deep smudges darkened his electric gray eyes, gilded by long lashes that should have made him look almost feminine. But the aquiline nose, with no fewer than two dents marring its aristocratic lineage, and the strong chin saved him from that. While his thinly sculpted upper lip hinted at the contempt she'd foolishly never seen before today, the lush lower lip spoke of the sensuality he hid beneath that ruthless mask.

She shivered slightly, even though his office was set to a comfortable ambient temperature.

The gray shirt revealed a teasing V of olive skin, skin Alex had kissed and petted to her heart's content. Her palm tingled in desperation for that contact again—to be able to slide her hand over his warm skin stretched taut over sculpted muscles. She'd thought it so romantic that she, with her always cold toes and fingers, had found a man who could warm her up just by holding her.

But even that reminder of her naive dreams couldn't stop her mind from imagining the slide of her hand moving farther down his defined chest to the thick slabs of his abdominal muscles, down to the solid strength of his thighs and then back up...

"Alessandra!"

Lost in the splendor that was the man she'd thought she had fallen headlong in love with, Alex said huskily, "Have I found what?"

He closed and opened his eyes, his patience apparently paper-thin. "What prompted you to come back? Did Greta promise to save you from the big, bad wolf? Did Leo and Massimo tell you they would protect you from the devious man you'd entangled yourself with?"

"I don't need anyone to fight my battles,"

Alex snapped, a fresh thread of anger thankfully drowning out the lust that was useless right now, that would only distract her from what she needed to do. "I have found myself in a situation where I… I—"

"You what?"

"I need you," she said, going for defiance but it ended up being an entreaty.

As if she'd woven a magic spell into the air, the very chemistry of the room changed. Like that first moment on Bali when their eyes had met, a real connection arced between them.

A pure electric charge that had nothing to do with revenge and all its twisted consequences. The luminous gray of his eyes flared into something dangerously feral and her pulse spiked.

God, was she really getting a thrill because she could still provoke this reaction from him? When would her stupid heart and her foolish body learn that he wasn't hers? That for all the pleasure he'd woven with his skillful caresses, he'd had an ultimate goal all the while?

"You need me for what, *bella*? I made the mistake of trusting you blindly once. I will not do it again."

The sheer arrogance of the words broke their connection. Alex laughed. "It's like you stole the very words from my script." She shook her head. If his gaze wasn't already drilling holes in her skin, she'd have smacked herself on the head. God, she needed him, yes, but for a good reason.

Not to dissolve into an overheated puddle at his feet.

"I need the appearance of this marriage," she announced clearly this time, tilting her chin up, holding his gaze. "That's why I returned."

His gaze irate, his jaw tight, he just stared at her.

"My mother and stepfather—" she swallowed the lump in her throat "—died in an accident two weeks ago." She didn't wait for him to offer a sentiment. If he showed any sympathy or touched her, her grief would come bursting out and she'd lose control of herself. And this situation. Never again was she going to depend on him. "I flew here straight from the funeral in San Francisco.

"My stepfather left a huge fortune to my half brother, Charlie. He's only seven and already his paternal uncles are fighting over who gets to take control of him. Just so they can control his fortune."

She blinked and turned away for a moment, trying to hold back the threat of tears.

"I'm sorry you've been dealing with such horrific news," he said, his voice coming close behind her. The scent of him was a tempting invitation, offering the illusion of an escape from her worries. "You didn't have to take it on alone, Alessandra."

The tenderness in his voice beckoned her, and it took all her strength to not fall into his embrace. To not let herself drown in grief. To not let his strong arms hold her through this pain.

She turned back to face him. "I kinda had to," she said vehemently, rejecting whatever comfort he was offering. "I've always dealt with life alone."

His mouth opened and closed, frustration etched onto his features. Long fingers pushed through his hair, sudden energy brimming from his demeanor. "Alessandra, I miscalculated how much what I—"

"I want to take custody of him," she said, cutting off his words. It was too late for apologies anyway. "I want to raise Charlie. I want to give him the kind of loving family life he deserves, the security I always yearned for as a child.

"Knowing how my stepfather's brothers are already fighting over him, as if he were a piece of meat, I can't give him up to them. I refuse to."

She looked up at him to realize she had his full attention. Thankful that he hadn't interrupted her again, she went on. "I've spoken to a firm of family lawyers that comes highly recommended. I've been informed in no uncertain terms that it's extremely unlikely I'd get custody of him with my current 'lifestyle.'

"I'm single, as far as anyone else knows. I travel around the world with no stability or roots.

I've been in the media spotlight a lot of late, creating controversy, and my breakup with Javier was messy and all over the news. In short, Charlie's uncles plan to use every morsel ever printed against me, even the smallest things I did ten years ago, to prove me an unfit guardian for him.

"So that's where you come in," she finished.

"Where?" His voice was whip sharp, his gaze cutting to her with a withering contempt that should've reduced her to a heap of smoking ash. "All I've heard so far is that you came back to me only because you were forced to do so. That something terribly tragic had to happen to make you show up here today. That your wedding vows still mean less than nothing to you.

"So where *exactly* do I come into this situation, *bella*. Spell it out for me."

Her behavior, so neatly summarized in his stinging words, made shame burn in her chest. But she buried it deep. She was never again going to project what she wanted to see in his eyes, what she wanted him to feel for her onto him. Never again.

"I'd already made a decision to quit modeling even before this happened. I plan to prove that I can be a steady, secure presence in Charlie's life, however long it takes. I plan to take the battle for custody to the courts and win it.

"It's just a matter of finishing up existing contracts, setting up a permanent residence somewhere and settling down to a less chaotic lifestyle. With my husband, so that I can prove to the courts that there's a stable, two-parent home waiting for Charlie."

"Is that all?" he said dryly.

"Yes, that is all," she snapped, fatigue finally taking over. "And since I already have a husband handy, I thought I should just use him to help my case."

"As opposed to?"

"As opposed to getting rid of the current one and shopping for a new one. What else?" she retorted, rolling her eyes. Her head was beginning to pound from all the lack of sleep, her body in a state of near exhaustion. "This is not a joke."

"Should I truly take you at your word this time, *bella*? Is that what I should have demanded—an extra clarification that it was not a joke when you made your vows to me?"

Alex refused to indulge the guilt that burrowed into the most private recesses of her heart. Or the hope that it had somehow hurt him when she'd left. God, the last thing she needed was to look for any supposed feelings for her. "You owe me this, V."

He raised a brow, arrogance dripping from the gesture. "Owe you, Princess?"

"Yes. You married me without telling me the whole truth. You appear to have conveniently forgotten all the mistakes you've made and blame me for the disturbing farce that is our marriage. You misrepresented yourself to me and I want reparation. This has to be it."

"I told you before. I'm saying it again. Our marriage is not a farce to me."

"I'm not asking you for a happily-ever-after, V." She cut him off, that tough mask in place again. "That's kind of lost its shine for me.

"I'm asking, since we're inconveniently tied together legally already, if you'll help me secure the happiness of a small boy who's just lost his parents and has been thrust into a battle between greedy adults who care only about the bottom line.

"If you were really once that boy who fought against overwhelming odds to survive, you will understand that a child's well-being is at stake here."

After the almost soap-opera-ish drama that had been his life recently, Vincenzo hadn't thought he'd ever be shocked again. But the fire that burned in Alessandra's eyes, the fighting stance of her body as she faced him, achieved that effect quite thoroughly.

This was the woman he'd lost his head over.

Vulnerable yet fierce.

Fragile and yet with a steely core.

In her, he'd seen a woman that would get behind him. A woman who'd have fought against all the injustices that had been done him. A woman who'd understand his lifelong fight, his ambition, his need to even out the scales. A woman—his *wife*—whom he'd thought would take his side against people who were not even her blood relations.

But he refused to be taken in by her again. Refused to let his heart rule over the little sense his head spouted. Refused to forget that, for all her determination now, she'd walked out on him, on their marriage, without even a word.

Worse, she wouldn't have returned if she hadn't been forced into it by a cruel twist of fate.

But for all his reservations, he couldn't remain untouched by the very real grief in her eyes, the guilt whenever she mentioned her mother, the hopelessness when she recounted how Charlie was being fought over.

All feelings he was too familiar with.

"Do you comprehend what an enormous responsibility you're taking on by seeking custody of Charlie?" he asked softly.

Her gaze jerked to meet his. "Yes." Calm. Steady.

"This is not an impulsive decision, is it? Because apparently you're the queen of impulsive behavior."

She fidgeted with the strap of her bag, bringing his gaze to her breasts, before weakly refuting, "That's not fair."

"I've gained a broader picture of you in the weeks you've been hiding, *cara*. Apparently, you have a history of making major, life-changing decisions on a whim."

A stiffness imbued her movements as she approached his desk and poured herself a glass of water. "I've no idea what you're talking about."

"Signing up to a modeling career—just because you knew your mother would disapprove.

"Walking out on a two-million-dollar contract with a cosmetics company because you discovered that their practices were not entirely ethical. Hiding from the fallout of that in Bali, which was when I found you. Then there's your decision to quit modeling altogether—for reasons unknown.

"And finally, marrying me on the rebound... because you got dumped by your ex," he said, giving voice to the thing that had bothered him the most.

Her almond-shaped eyes widened. "Javier again?"

"Oh no, this is all according to Massimo. He's been quite voluble in your absence, volunteering information about you at regular intervals. Exacting his own version of revenge on me, I'd say."

"Revenge?"

"He knew how...angry I was by your middle-of-the-night flight. So he dealt me a few punches and got some laughs out of it." Massimo, Vincenzo had realized in the past few weeks, found him endlessly fascinating, as if he were a puzzle the tech genius was determined to solve.

It was damned hard to hate a man who kept dropping down into his office for little chats as if they were childhood friends. Or, God forbid, long-lost brothers. Not even on pain of death would Vincenzo admit, however, that he was just as curious about the cyber tech genius.

"So, is it true?"

"Is what true?" she asked.

Vincenzo had a feeling she was playing with him. And yet he couldn't help gritting out the question that had been gouging a hole in him for nine excruciatingly long weeks. "Did you marry me on the rebound, Princess?"

The little minx fluttered her eyes at him, sweetly pretending to consider the question while his insides tightened into a knot. "You know, there might be some truth to that after all. How else can I explain the temporary madness that took hold of me in Bali? Javi and I…had such grand plans together and then it all fell apart so spectacularly. My relationship had failed. My career held no thrill any longer.

"I found myself hiding in Bali, devastated by everything that had shifted beneath my feet and then there you were… Prince Charming, running to my rescue.

"Except you're more like the slimy, cold-blooded frog than the prince."

His jaw tightened and Alex knew she'd landed a solid hit.

She straightened as he came to her, his voice deceptively soft when he spoke. "You've just been through a terrible loss. Grief and guilt should not be the motivators to involve yourself in a child's life. He's not something you can return to a shop when the fancy wears off."

The sudden change to this most serious of topics, and offering his sensible opinion stole the ground from underneath her. The complex facets to this man amazed her, and the surprises kept hitting her just when she thought she had the measure of him.

He smiled thinly. "You're shocked that a man like me—ruthless, cold, cruel even—can think of a child's well-being in this situation, can see beyond our petty differences, *si*?"

"No. Yes, I mean… I didn't think you'd be quite so rational about it." She shrugged. "It gives me hope that I'm not pushing Charlie from one horrible situation to another. Even if it is only temporary."

"You have considered that I might be a different but just as horrible situation for him then?"

"Of course I have. You lied to me. You've lost my trust. I thought long and hard over that before I came back to you today."

"And what did you conclude?"

"My first step is to get custody of Charlie.

Once I achieve that goal, once this marriage becomes nothing but a liability to me, I'll—"

"You'll do away with me?" he said, a glint of wicked humor gleaming in his eyes.

Alex shrugged, a small smile playing around her own mouth. "Something like that, yes."

His gaze turned thoughtful, as he stood there caging her with his body. She could almost hear the gears turning in that Machiavellian mind of his. "*Bene*, I'll play along for the world. But I have a price for my cooperation."

"Of course you do." She glared at him. "It seems you're nothing if not predictable."

"You're asking me to take on an important role in the life of a child—"

"I'm not asking you to be a permanent parent to him—"

"Ah…how do you see this playing out, then?" he asked, parodying the question she'd asked of him. "We pretend to be an adoring couple, you get custody of your half brother and then you run off to some quiet corner of the world with him in tow, never to be seen again and forget all about your poor husband?"

There was no place in the world she could go to where she could outrun her feelings for him. "What's your price, V?" she demanded, facing him, refusing to back down even though everything inside her was building to an unbearably heightened sense of unwanted anticipation.

He tucked his finger under her chin and looked her straight in the eye. "The same as always, Alessandra."

"Spell it out for me."

"I've only ever wanted what was mine. No more, no less.

"I want the wife you promised me you'd be. I want the marriage that this was supposed to be. I want you to stand by my side while I achieve the goal I've worked toward all my life."

"Those promises were made based on false assumptions. You're not the man I thought you were. And nothing will make me betray Leo and Massimo."

Impatience glittered in his eyes. "You do them a disservice, *cara*. Leonardo and Massimo can look after themselves. Charlie can't. Why don't you focus your energies on him?"

"You make it sound so simple. As if everything sits in a different compartment—"

"You don't seem to grasp one crucial thing. Whether I had seen you in Bali or not, whether or not I had thrown all my own rules out the window and married you when I've never even had a girlfriend for more than two months, this was always going to be my path in life, Alessandra.

"I would still have done everything I could to ruin all that bears the name Brunetti."

"And I'll be damned before I let you use me against them," she threw back at him.

Vincenzo took her in, reluctant admiration and pride building up in his chest.

From the portrait Massimo had drawn of her, from her own actions in the last nine weeks, he'd wondered at the sanity of what he'd done. If he'd been taken in by her beauty and his lust. But now, he knew he'd made the right decision.

He wanted this Alessandra that fought for the people she loved in her life so ferociously. He wanted that loyalty all for himself.

And whether cruel or not, fate had given him another chance with her. Alessandra's resolve to do the right thing by her half brother was his chance, his opportunity to set things straight between them.

An opportunity to get her to spend time with him, to make her see his side of the story. To turn this temporary arrangement she'd suggested into the permanent marriage he still wanted.

"Fine, I'll give you what you're asking for. We will pretend to be a happy, blissfully in love couple for the world. I will help you win custody of Charlie. After a trial period of say three months."

"Trial period of what exactly?"

"Of you behaving yourself."

"Behaving myself? How dare you—"

"Hear me out, Alessandra. You say I've broken your trust? You have done exactly the same to me. Believe me, Princess, you're the first person

I gave that to and you threw it back in my face without a single moment's doubt."

The thin thread of resentment in those words killed Alex's ready argument. Words fell away from her lips as she stared at him, a simple truth emerging from all of it.

Their marriage had meant something to him. Maybe not the same thing as it had to her. But something. And her walking out on it, on him, he saw as...what? Abandonment? A betrayal? Had this marriage, his vows, really been sacred to him?

"I won't... I can't let you bring a child into this thing between us without ensuring it is truly what you want. That you'll see all this through— these huge decisions and being a parent—without running away from it. For three months, don't make any more life-changing decisions. Deal with your grief over your mother's loss. Decide what you want to do with your career."

She hated that he was being the sensible one here. "There's nothing to deal with, V."

"You've just lost your mother, Princess. You—"

"I never really had my mother in the first place to lose her."

He reached for her hand but Alex instinctively jerked away from him. Because she didn't trust herself. Not with him.

He exhaled roughly. "Don't run away. Don't… Just stay still, with me. Show the world that you're settling down. Show me that you're committed to this arrangement over the next three months. And then we'll start the custody proceedings."

"But that's three months that Charlie's…"

"Visit with him in the meantime. Wrap up your other obligations. Three months is a small drop in the ocean when you consider the fact that you'll give him a stable home for the rest of his life."

"Three months is a long time to a child who's just lost everything, who's living with family members who see him as nothing but a meal ticket to a better life. You're doing this just to punish me. Because I walked out on you."

"No, Alessandra. I'm doing this to make sure we both know what we're getting into this time. To make sure we're not compounding the first mistake by bringing an innocent into this mess."

"Both you and I know how much damage could be done to a child by the smallest thoughtless action. We can't…" Her throat caught on the words. "I can't leave him there alone, unprotected."

"Fine, Princess," Vincenzo offered in a soothing tone. His brow furrowed into a thoughtful frown while he stared at her with that same intensity he brought to everything he did. "Did your mother have any friends that Charlie knows well?"

"Yes." Alex nodded.

"People you trust?"

"Yep. They have a little boy Charlie's age. I met them when I visited him for his last birthday party."

"You said you and your mother were estranged."

Alex shrugged. "Yes, we were. But that doesn't mean I was going to completely shut Charlie out of my life. I never missed a birthday of his, and as soon as he learned to read, I regularly sent him little cards and letters."

"I'll make some calls. Maybe we can arrange for him to stay with that family until the custody hearing is done. He can go to the same school as their son, keep the same routine and have familiar people around him while you and I figure this out."

Alex nodded, gratitude cutting away any words that could rise up and ruin this temporary détente. At least in this matter, her trust in him hadn't been misplaced. And he was right.

She'd run away from her problems in the past. More than once. But not anymore.

This time, she was going to face them, and him, head-on.

She was going to stay by his side and do everything she could to stop this destruction of the Brunettis that he was bent on, using every weapon available to her. But never again was she going to forget that there was a bone-deep ruthlessness inside him; never again was she going to foolishly believe that he was capable of love.

"I have a condition of my own too," she threw at him impulsively, the idea of three months living in close quarters with him seeming like a lifetime. A lifetime of intimacy, of awareness and desire, of shattered dreams and naive hopes.

"What?" he said smoothly, even as he uncoiled himself and sauntered toward her. It was like watching a predator emerge from stalking, ready to pounce.

She stood rooted in place, refusing to reveal how much his nearness affected her. How much the heat of his body called to her. "I'm not sleeping with you. This is not a real marriage. Not anymore."

"Ah… Massimo was right."

Her breath stuttered in her throat as he lifted his hand and gently pushed away a strand of her hair from her shoulder. "About what?"

"That I don't know you well at all. But even he doesn't know how cruel you can be, does he, Princess?"

Alex compulsively licked her lips just as his gaze zeroed in there. "It muddies everything for me. That's how you trapped me in the first place. You're too damned good in bed."

A wicked light came into his eyes, making them magnetic. "I think that's just the connection between us, *bella*. A connection that you're doing everything to run away from."

"Hot sex, however tempting, can't be the only bedrock of a marriage."

"Unfortunately for my body, I agree." He pursed his lips and leveled a thoughtful look at her. "Shall I suggest an amendment to your condition?"

"What?"

"We should each be allowed to try to seduce the other, *si*? If I try and you give in, you can't hold that against me."

"I won't give in. And I definitely don't want to seduce you."

He tilted his head to the side, his gaze holding hers captive. "Then there's no harm in the challenge then, is there?" She had somehow managed to nod when he bent his head and whispered in her ear. "I do wish you'd change your mind about seducing me, Princess."

Her heart raced, sensation zinging across her skin. "Why?"

"There's nothing more arousing, nothing sexier in the world than a beautiful, powerhouse of a woman who goes after what she wants with a single-minded determination.

"In fact, I'd say that's how *you trapped me*, Princess." His lips never really grazed the sensitive skin beneath her ear, but Alex felt the touch nevertheless, like a searing burn. "Being so thoroughly wanted like that by you is an incredible high unlike any other in the entire world."

CHAPTER FIVE

ALESSANDRA HATED TO admit it, even during the most peaceful moments while she'd been hiding out in Bali, but there had been a kernel of doubt in her mind as to whether she'd done the right thing in deciding to quit modeling.

Show after high stakes frantic show for top designers around the world, running from city to city, country to country like a nomad, working close to eighty hours a week, with no time for a personal life or the deep commitments she'd wanted—the stress of it had taken its toll on her.

Of course, she'd partied in the beginning—partied hard with the heady freedom of a six-teen-year-old who'd found the world at her feet—but over the years the vacuous, often cut-throat glamor of it all had paled and she'd become more and more unhappy.

Photographers who'd once loved working with her had started calling her fractious, restless, the second she hadn't been performing to perfection. She'd been turning up late for fitting appointments, finding a myriad of excuses. Once she'd arrived late and covered in glitter and hair spray from a previous show, minutes before she was due to walk, the stress of running across the city during fashion week making her nauseous. Making her want to run away from the sea of frantic strangers surrounding her.

That particular evening, she'd confided in Javier that her heart just wasn't in it anymore.

The creep had mocked her. From there, their argument had spiraled into a complete destruction of their relationship, the only place it had left to go. Only then had she realized she didn't want to be with Javier. He had become another crutch.

And then she'd learned the appalling facts about the working conditions of the cosmetics company she represented. Horrified, Alex had scathingly criticized the company in an interview and quit the contract on the spot.

It had been a hotheaded, more than reckless, move. Her agent had blasted her—she was gathering too much ill will in an industry where reputation meant everything. Even the warning hadn't been enough to make her care.

She'd had enough. So she had run off to Bali and ended up marrying the first man who'd shown an interest in her.

Seen like that, the picture of her that emerged didn't look good.

Now, while she stood like a mannequin with

her arms stretched out, her face upturned for a makeup artist to dab highlighter onto her cheeks, Alex looked at her reflection in the mirror under the overhead lights and smiled.

Relief was a river gushing through her insides.

God, she was so done with this.

Only a few minutes to the show and backstage was packed with people, all to ensure a fabulous show. She was totally aware of the strange looks she'd been getting from all of them, ever since she'd arrived.

Gossip was the backbone of the fashion industry, and she'd no doubt her stunt with the cosmetics company, her subsequent absence for the last few months and her sudden reappearance now were the hot topics of discussion.

She felt free, as if a weight had been lifted, as she shrugged on a sheer, lacy, red cover-up and moved to join the line of models about to go on.

Someone sidled up to the producer, Isha, who was one of Alex's few friends in the industry, and a heated argument ensued. All heads turned to them as both women bent their head over a seating arrangement.

Alex sidled up to her friend in the wings and enveloped her in a side hug, being extra careful as to not smudge her makeup or even breathe the wrong way. "Everything okay?"

"Some big *bajillionaire* VIP has shown up, un-announced, at the last minute, and his team of assistants wants a front row seat for him, of course. Even the crazy genius that is Jean Benoit," she said, mentioning the designer whose collection they were showing off, "doesn't want to get on this man's wrong side. They're all turning themselves inside out figuring out where to put him.

"Apparently, he's here to see one of the models."

Alex felt a flutter of alarm in her chest. It had been a fortnight since Vincenzo and she had butted heads, then agreed to a plan. Since they both had super busy schedules, they'd barely seen each other since. It suited her just fine, even though she knew the logistics of their deal would come at her soon enough like a freight train.

Suddenly, Alex understood how a hunted animal felt. "Any idea who it is?"

Isha shook her head. "Focus on the show, Alex."

The flutter morphed into a full-blown panic attack. "Isha, just tell me."

"It's the same Italian businessman—the reclusive owner of that international brokerage firm who's been in the media spotlight the past week. It was leaked that he's related to the Brunettis of Milan, which is why he's been going after them. Apparently, he's the secret illegitimate son of the old coot, Silvio. His name's…"

"Vincenzo Cavalli," Alex added, her insides turning into spaghetti. Her heart thumped with a dizzying excitement, and it had nothing to do with the high she usually associated with doing a show.

Alex squared her shoulders and strutted out onto the catwalk, wondering how apt the song blaring out of the speakers was.

Something about bad girls living fast and burning out.

She had to be if she wanted to change the mind of the man sitting in the middle seat of the front row, eating her alive with those penetrating gray eyes.

Too late to back out now that she'd made a deal with the devil.

Vincenzo threw back the last bit of his whiskey and walked up the curving designer staircase onto the balcony that offered a bird's-eye view of the latest nonstop party central that was the nightclub he'd launched recently.

Seeing the final product tonight, when it had been the ruins of an old, abandoned train depot not long ago, filled him with an immense satisfaction.

The secret nightclub—not so secret anymore now that the high fashion crowd of Milan had discovered it—was bustling with people from the show. Hip-hop music blared through the loudspeakers, while bartenders delighted the crowds with colorful cocktails.

But even with purple strobe lights flashing on and off from crowd to crowd, he could still spot his dear little wife.

His gaze unerringly returned to Alessandra again and again, desperate to drink in the sight of her after two weeks of drought.

He'd always been a man who took risks. A man who played against the odds and won. Or else he wouldn't have been in a position to challenge the Brunetti brothers, who'd been born with every conceivable advantage.

His marriage had been a risk, just like this club had been, but not a strategic or financial risk like all the others. It had been a different kind. But in the end, it would pay out.

Alessandra fluttered through the party like a butterfly, flitting from flower to flower. Her toned, curvaceous body that she maintained with an iron-willed discipline showcased beautifully in the slinky black number that parted with a wide V-neck, displaying the sides of her breasts, and yet somehow remained tasteful, elegant. There was a slight ruffled hem that flirted around her upper thighs, again just about covering those round buttocks he'd cradled in his palms a few months ago.

No such contact was forthcoming anytime soon, he realized with a self-deprecating smile. He'd just have to be patient. He'd have to win Alessandra like he did everything else in life.

Knowing that the woman he'd married was an international supermodel that men fantasized over was one thing. Seeing it in person was another. It felt like every man here at the club had swarmed her.

"Everyone adores Alessandra."

Here was proof. And yet she'd chosen to marry him after knowing him only for a few short weeks.

"I'm not a prize, Vincenzo."

Her angry words reverberated inside his head, and he knew he was wrong for feeling this sense of pride whenever he saw her.

An atavistic response, uncharacteristic and unworthy of him. Mine, something inside him insisted. *Only mine.*

He frowned, as a particularly tenacious man followed her from group to group, an urgency to his swarthy features. A stocky Spaniard by the name of Javier Diaz, Vincenzo had no doubt.

He kept an eye on them, ready to lend help if needed, but she dismissed her ex with a scathing remark that had her eyes flashing sparks. That made Vincenzo smile despite the tension stiffening his shoulders.

Other than a brief tilt of her head in acknowledgment, she'd been avoiding Vincenzo all evening.

He let her.

She needed to decompress after the electrifying atmosphere of the show and the relentless demands it had placed on her, and he… He needed to get a better handle on his own emotions tonight before he approached her.

While he'd intended to give them both a breathing space and the energy to finish their immediate obligations before the media ruckus the announcement of their marriage would cause— two fashion shows and one photoshoot in Alessandra's case—and everything had gone to hell. Someone had leaked his relationship to the Brunettis to the press.

He'd had to cut his Beijing trip short to deal with the media circus and the crisis it had caused with the BFI board.

"Is it true that Silvio Brunetti seduced a hotel maid and you were the product?"

"Are you the illegitimate son of Silvio Brunetti?"

"What are your intentions for BFI?"

The Brunetti Bastard one trashy tabloid had called him, choosing to go with the lowest denominator.

Upon arriving at the HQ of BFI this morning, there had been further challenges to deal with. He wondered if it was Alessandra who'd leaked the news, causing him considerable damage.

The fallout with the two board members he'd had in his pocket, had set him back almost two months of careful negotiations. Considerable speculation had been raised as to how and why he'd started taking over the board of BFI. Exactly how he had gained ownership of Silvio Brunetti's stock.

He'd arrived at the fashion show, temper frayed, determined to confront the woman whose loyalty should've been to him. Only him.

Instead, seeing her strutting on the catwalk, challenge and confidence oozing from every pore, her body a finely honed machine, her eyes glowing with some inner zeal had completely undercut his anger.

Alessandra in that bloodred bikini top—some sort of studded corset that propped up her already high breasts—and a thong in the same color, with light brown high heels that almost blended into her skin, and all that golden-brown hair pulled back into a tight bun that sharpened her already flawless bone structure, was never going to leave his memory bank even if he lived to be a hundred.

Her red lipstick had made her pouty mouth a lesson in sensuality and sin.

The woman had far too much power over him, moving him from anger to laughter to desire as if he were a windup toy she could turn on and off at her leisure.

She looked up at that precise moment, the flashing purple lights lighting up her lithe body, her eyes shimmering with naked challenge.

Something inside him awakened with a growl.

Because this woman, who challenged him, who was making him work for her loyalty, whose surrender would be so delicious when he finally won it, she set his blood on fire. And he'd had enough of watching her from a distance, like those other besotted men. Enough of pussyfooting around her because of misplaced guilt about hurting her. Enough of trying to give her space and time to deal with her grief.

The world needed to know that she belonged to him. That she had thrown her lot in with him. The explosive news that Alessandra Giovanni had married the Brunetti Bastard should be enough to gain him back some of the ground he'd lost this past week.

It should have been all about damage control at this point. But the thought of winning his wife over fired his blood like nothing else.

Leaning his forearms on the wrought iron balustrade, Vincenzo held her gaze. And beckoned her upstairs with his index finger. Laughter broke out of him at the dawning effrontery in her expression, a fire in his veins as he imagined those beautiful brown eyes clouding over with passion when she eventually surrendered to him.

He was a man used to surrender, and he would accept nothing less from the woman he'd married.

Apparently, whatever reprieve she'd been offered over the last two weeks was finally over. Foolish of her to hope he'd disappear after the fashion show without seeking her out.

He stood on the balcony, looking down upon her, his gray gaze perusing her with such an intense possessiveness that she felt owned.

How dare he beckon her with a finger, as if she were his puppet!

And yet, here she was, answering his summons. Their encounters in Bali had hinted at a depth of emotion that she didn't see in most men.

Greta had really lost it with Alex, calling her a naive, besotted fool for not realizing his true nature. But she'd been so sure about him. If there was one thing she'd had exposure to from the ripe age of sixteen, it was men.

She'd been hit on, propositioned, come on to, even harassed, by everyone from a lowly lighting manager to a megarich designer, to a CEO of a multinational corporation.

Most men were either intimidated by the idea of all that she was and tried to overcompensate for it in various ways. Others—usually rich investment types—thought that all it took to impress her was a bigger fortune than hers and a bigger ego.

But Vincenzo hadn't fallen into either camp. He had been different from that very first moment.

There had been something very down-to-earth about him, an awareness of his place in the world and the power he could wield. Respect that he offered her immediately for the basic reason that she was another human being, a sense of reserve that she'd been itching to topple from the first time he'd walked her to her villa and then walked away without presuming anything.

She hadn't been wrong about the fact that here was a man who felt deeply about things. Who had more emotional bandwidth than anyone she'd ever been involved with.

Only all that emotion had been deliberately channeled, for years and years, in a bitter quest for revenge, to destroy the people she loved most. And she meant to sway him from that path...

No wonder Leo had thought she was in over her head. Massimo had simply smiled, winked and asked her to load herself up with dynamite for she was trying to move a mountain.

She took the final step and immediately regretted leaving the safety of the crowd behind. The space beyond him was expansive but cut away from the prying eyes of others. Too much privacy. Too many secluded corners with dark leather couches that could swallow up a newly married couple who hadn't touched each other in months.

"You're not my lord and master," she said tartly. Drumming up her defenses.

"And yet here you are."

"I didn't think this was the time to engage in that particular battle."

"Ah...so you do know your limits."

"What limits?"

"You know you've pushed me far enough already, *si*?" he asked huskily, stepping from the shadows into the light. "Do you want to sit?"

"No, I don't. I wouldn't like to sit." She lowered her voice, realizing he'd moved even closer. The lemony scent of him swept through her, evoking a piercing shaft of need. "I like standing. In fact, I haven't done enough of it today. I—"

"We don't have to do anything you don't want to do, Alessandra," he said, his baritone voice going all deep and low and smoky, just the way it did when he was aroused. When he wrapped those skillful hands around her. When he moved inside of her.

But there was something else too.

Pulling in a deep breath, she finally let herself look at him. The dark leather jacket he'd worn to the show had been discarded. His gunmetal gray dress shirt was unbuttoned and uncuffed, giving her a glimpse of the chest hair that had the most incredible effect when rubbed against her own naked skin...

A lazy smile split his mouth, crinkling at the edges of his eyes, shooting straight through to her heart. The damned man was laughing at her.

"You look quite flushed, *cara mia*. Maybe a cold drink will help."

She did feel overheated, even the soft lace of her dress feeling far too tight. She clenched her hands around the cool metal of the balcony. "I'm fine. Stop being so…"

So irresistible. So knee-meltingly gorgeous. So blatantly masculine.

"So what?"

"So…solicitous. As if—" She shook her head far too forcefully, and her hair tumbled down from the loose knot she'd put it in, the brown clip clinking against the cool marble floor. Swearing, she bent down, but he got there first. "Thanks," she said, extending her hand, but he pulled away.

"Leave it like that."

"I don't want to—" she pulled the heavy weight away from her neck "—and it's too—"

"The entire world gets to see you strut down the catwalk in a bikini that's been designed to fire up every red-blooded man's fantasies, *bella*, and that's fine with me." His gaze took in the thrust of her breasts as she held up the swathe of her hair, the pulse hammering away at her throat, the swipe of her tongue against her trembling lower lip. His eyes met hers with a naked hunger that was a balm to her wounded ego. "But do not deny me my fantasies, Alessandra.

"All I've wanted for the past two weeks is to see you sprawled on my bed, that hair spread out on my pillow, but clearly that's not going to happen anytime soon, no? This is the least you can do to keep your poor husband going. Even as you thrust a knife into my back, Princess."

The feral possessiveness of his voice was like a thunderbolt filling her veins with an electric sizzle. "A knife into your back?" she said, her words breathy, distracted.

"You *have* been a bad girl, *bella*. Helping out the defenseless Brunetti men."

The edge to his words made Alex frown. "I don't know what you're talking about."

He tilted his head, considering her thoughtfully. "You're going to persuade me that it wasn't you who leaked my dirty beginnings to the tabloids? That dented my reputation in the financial circles of Milan?"

She stared at him, aghast. "The last thing I'd do now is lie to you. I think there's been enough of that between us already, don't you?"

"You're magnificent even when you attack me, Princess."

"You're gorgeous even when you're being Machiavellian, V."

He laughed and those crinkles appeared again. And it was damned impossible to hold herself at arm's length when she badly wanted to melt into his broad frame and beg him to walk away from all this.

To put their relationship first. To put their future first. To put *her* first.

"I didn't leak it, V. Whether you believe me or not is up to you. You might not think twice about hurting people but that's not how I operate. Especially when I can understand how painful it must have been to be that innocent child.

"I've thrown my lot in with you. At least for the near future."

He held her gaze in the flickering light for a long while and finally nodded. "Then it has to have been your lovely stepmother, Greta."

"That's an unfair jump. You're determined to see them all as your enemies."

"Who else benefits by it?" he pointed out. "I'll admit that it was a clever move on her part, that it set me back quite a bit."

"What? How?"

"I lost the support of two members of the BFI board who'd been ready to throw their vote behind me instead of Leo. Stock prices for Cavalli Enterprises have been plummeting ever since the news hit the papers.

"*The Brunetti Bastard* has quite the ring to it, *si*? A clever little moniker."

"Of course it's not," Alex replied, the latent bitterness in his words shaking her up. That his plans had been set back gave her no satisfaction in the face of his hurt. But… "Has it made any difference, V?" she couldn't help asking.

His head jerked up. "Difference to what?"

"To see yourself from a different perspective.

"Face what you've done, what you're doing publicly, going against ethical businessmen like Leo and Massimo, against a revered institution like BFI that they've rebuilt into something of value.

"Shouldn't it at least make you pause and reconsider what you—"

"You think I care what the world's perception of me is? Or that I've been only half-awake for the past two decades while I planned and plotted against them using every weakness I could find to further my cause? You think I can stop now, after all these years?"

She blinked, feeling as if she'd been dropped onto the concrete floor of reality with a bruising thud. But she refused to look away. Refused to back down. "If I can stop running from my life, then you can—"

"Enough, Alessandra! Let it be."

He looked away from her into the crowd. "You didn't last long before you broke our agreement, did you?"

She frowned. "Our agreement, which you just dictated by the way, was that I don't make impulsive, life-altering decisions in the next three months. Standing mutely by your side while you take down people I care about is... Well, let's just say that will never be me. Honestly, it's not like

I have any ammunition against you. All I have are words."

"I'm glad you think that," he said, with a self-deprecation that had her jerking her head up. "You were…brilliant, glowing on the stage today. I can see why the fashion world is bemoaning you leaving the industry."

"My modeling career grounded me when I was directionless, true. But I'm done with it." She cleared her throat when he looked up. "It was an impulsive decision initially, I admit. I was disgusted by the working conditions that the cosmetic company was using. But it was just the catalyst I needed.

"I was tired of the constant grind, the relentless probing into my private life…the loneliness behind the bright lights was consuming me."

"What about that one?" He tilted his head toward the dance floor.

Alex didn't have to look down to see who he meant. For a minute, she dallied with the idea of embellishing her relationship with Javi just to save her pride. Just to make Vincenzo feel a little unsure of where he stood with her. Wanted to see the flash of jealousy she'd seen that day when he'd asked if he was a rebound for her.

She discarded the idea in the next. Lies and deception had never been her thing.

"Things hadn't been right between us for a long time. When I told him that I was considering walking away from it all, he revealed his true colors. His use for me was going to be considerably reduced once I stepped out of the limelight."

She shrugged, even though a part of her still hurt. It had been a long time since she'd indulged in the fantasy that Javi and she shared some big, romantic love, but to learn that for him all her value lay in her modeling career was still a bitter pill to swallow. Just like discovering that she'd only been a duty to her mother—a necessary punishment for the sin she'd committed in having an extramarital fling with Alex's father.

"He's still sniffing around you."

"I was spectacular today, like you said. So Javi's wondering if he let me go too soon."

"After that fight, you dumped him instantly and hightailed it to Bali, *si*?"

"Something like that, yes. But on that occasion my impulse was absolutely right. Realizing that I'm at the tail end of this career now, that retirement is truly what I want at this point in my life...that gave me that extra sparkle on the stage tonight.

"I'm going to finish at the top. No regrets. No looking back as I start the next chapter of my life."

"You sound determined," he said quietly.

"Enough to convince you that I mean this?"

"Si." He straightened from the lazy pose and every cell in her stood up to attention. "Maybe I can suggest the first paragraph in the new chapter? It's time to reveal the little secret of our marital status to the world, don't you think?"

"I guess."

"What better venue than now? Tonight?"

"Okay, yeah," she said, casting a look around the huge, packed nightclub.

It hadn't gone unnoticed that he'd summoned her and she'd answered the arrogant summons. One look at their body language would be more than enough for anyone to see that their interest in each other was anything but platonic. "Most big media outlets have someone down there. What were you thinking? A statement as we walk out?"

After what felt like an eternity, he covered the short distance between them, his arrogant stare taking on an edge of something else. Another step and their thighs grazed just a little.

Alex shivered, every inch of her body, desperate for contact, bowing toward him. His fingers landed on her temple, pushing the mass of her hair from her face. And then he cupped the back of her neck gently. Giving her a chance to step away. "I was thinking a kiss, right here. Stir up some interest before we announce the pertinent facts."

Music hammered around them. The intimate contact, after the drought of so many months, felt like a spark of fire in her body. She was going to say yes. She knew it. He knew it. The hungry denizens of the press were just a reason they were both using. Except she didn't want to be the one who gave in too easily. Who blinked first.

She ran her fingers through her hair and fluttered her lashes at him. "You're doing this to punish me for walking out on you." She pouted, knowing that the particular red she was wearing tonight made her mouth look like a tart strawberry.

"I didn't realize kissing me was such a punishment, *bella*."

She bent her mouth closer to his ear. "It isn't. In fact, there's very few things in life I enjoy more. And you know that. That's the punishment. To be reminded of how helpless I am to this… thing between us even when I don't trust you."

A vein pulsed in his temple. "All I want is to kiss my wife after months of going to bed alone, wishing she was there to welcome me. Of waking up alone in the middle of the night fully aroused, but knowing that no relief is forthcoming except by my hand. While wondering if I had imagined how bloody good it had been when you came to me that first time in Bali and I took you under the stars in the night sky."

"It was that good," she added simply. Wishing she was the type that could play games. Wishing she could somehow use his attraction to her, that desperate huskiness of his tone, to her advantage.

But she couldn't. "Okay. Let's get it over with."

"That sounds like you're bracing yourself for battle."

"You don't think the battle's already begun?"

"I guess you will claim I started it?"

"Yes."

"And must I finish the battle too?"

"No. I will. You should know, though, that I intend to win. At any cost."

"All I wanted was a peaceful marriage with a biddable woman," he said, with a put-upon sigh.

Laughter roared out of her, melting away the stress and grief of the past few months, at least for a moment. This was the man she'd fallen for in that lush island paradise. This man who'd laughed with her, who'd teased her. Who'd listened to her talking about her dreams.

He didn't quite laugh with her but his eyes gleamed in the darkness. In the flickering light and shadows of the club, the lines of his face looked astonishingly beautiful. "And the prize for winning?"

"There's a prize?"

"There's always a prize in these things. Shall I tell you what it is, Princess?" he whispered, his breath hot against her lips, his arrogant nose flaring.

Alex placed her open palms against his chest. His heart thundered under her fingers, the beat steadily rising as she leaned her thighs against the rock-hard cradle of his. Heat. Hardness. Hunger. His maleness was an ocean she wanted to drown in. "What?" she croaked.

"Surrender."

"Never," she declared just as arrogantly, his very words imbuing her blood with challenge.

She pushed her palm up, up until she reached his neck. Sneaking her fingers into the thick hair at the nape of his neck, she tilted her head. His breath drew a hot path down her cheek, the scent of him a trigger her body instantly associated with long, lazy nights and indescribable pleasure.

Her other hand she kept on his abdomen, loving the tight clench and release of those powerful muscles every time she touched him.

"Not unless…"

"Not unless what?"

Slowly, she pressed her lips to his, pressing his head down with her fingers. As if he'd been made for the express purpose of pleasuring her. "Unless I take you down with me."

"Is that what you want?"

"Yes. I want to make you drown. In me. Until you can't tell what's right and wrong anymore. Until…"

Soft lips met hers in a rush of warmth and rollicking hunger. Alex drew a sizzling trail along the seam of that sensuous mouth with her tongue, her breath a labored hiss against his bristly jaw.

The remembered taste of him was like a detonation going off inside her body.

She nipped and kissed, licked and played with his mouth, but it wasn't enough.

Nowhere near enough.

She sneaked her tongue into his mouth on the next swipe. Pleasure exploded in sweet rivulets down her body as the taste of him filled her. Whiskey and want—he was all solid and real. And after the roller coaster of the last few months, here was the thing that had anchored her. She devoured him as if the taste of him on her tongue, the solid breadth of him in her hands, the labored rush of his breaths on her skin could fill the emptiness inside of her. As if he was all she needed.

Pressing herself into him, she took his mouth with a feral hunger. She licked and nipped, bit and laved at the pillowy lushness of his lips. Thrust in and out of his mouth in a rhythm she desperately needed to be feeling somewhere else.

His other hand landed on flesh where the slinky black number bared the curve of her hips. Those long fingers she knew so well fluttered over her skin, tender like butterfly wings, and yet leaving a wake of heat in their trail. "Slow down, *cara*. I'm not going anywhere," he whispered against her skin.

The dry humor in those words was a cold slap to her senses. Alex pulled away from him, her breaths choppy, the lack of solid warmth in her hands painfully real.

But for all the silky control of his words, she could see the stamp of desire on his tight features, the sharp hiss of his breath as he wrestled himself back under control, the curse he bit out when he moved.

"I think that's enough of a PDA to announce our marriage, *si*?" she whispered.

He grunted his assent and she laughed. But as they made their way downstairs, the caged passion of his body sliding deliciously against her own, answering the questions thrown their way, Alex wondered how a win could feel so much like a loss.

CHAPTER SIX

AN UNCOMMONLY BRISK September breeze plastered her silk blouse and long skirt against her body as Alex stood waiting on the steps outside the Brunetti villa.

Her temper matched the wind's bite. God, she was surrounded by the most infuriatingly stubborn people on the face of the planet.

The roar of the Lamborghini Aventador had cut short her rapid-fire argument with Greta, who'd refused to even contemplate the idea of apologizing to Vincenzo. As much as it galled Alex to acknowledge it of the woman who had welcomed her with open arms, Greta's actions toward Vincenzo and his mother all those years ago had been thoughtless at best and cruel at worst. Even Massimo had blasted Greta for it.

It didn't matter that at that time, Greta had been doing her best to corral her son, Silvio—an egotistical monster bent on destroying the revered institution that was BFI as well as Massimo and Leo's lives. Neither was Greta willing to understand that Alex's marriage to Vincenzo wasn't a momentary madness that she could simply walk away from right now.

On the other side was Vincenzo, using their intimate, spine-melting kiss at the nightclub, using every detail of their relationship to enable him to continue his siege on BFI. Whatever setback the article in the press had initially caused him, he was using their "fairy-tale-esque romance" to clean up his image.

It was bad enough that Leo's own reputation as BFI's CEO had taken a hit after Vincenzo's sustained attacks for over a year now. And now the news of his marriage to her... Alex could almost see the neat twist.

If Alessandra Giovanni—the adopted daughter of the Brunettis—had fallen head over heels for Vincenzo Cavalli, he couldn't be all that bad, could he?

The press had turned the untamable wolf that was Vincenzo Cavalli into the most romantic man on the planet.

Alex pursed her mouth as the purring engine of the Aventador came to a smooth halt in front of her. Her pulse spiked as Vincenzo stepped out and walked around to her side.

In a V-necked sweater and denim that sinfully molded to those hard thighs, he looked like every sinful temptation she'd ever had. His jet-black hair had a wet sheen from the shower, his freshly shaven jaw all sharp angles. Looking composed was hard when all she wanted to do was press her face against the exposed skin at his throat and absorb some much-needed warmth.

The media had exploded after their kiss and the subsequent reveal of their wedding, but they still hadn't worked out all the logistics of where they would live. She was still finishing up her last contracts, talking to Charlie every day and playing out the social circuit in Milan with Vincenzo by her side.

Not that she didn't welcome the reprieve it gave her. Resisting him was a much easier concept when they parted ways at the end of the night.

Leaning against the Aventador, he looked effortlessly urbane, sophisticated in a raw, powerful way. Not even the most gorgeous male models she'd known could achieve that confidence, that wicked arrogance without a lot of practice.

Here was a man who did not need his ego to be stroked. Or pandered to, in any way. Who had earned everything he possessed the hard way.

His gaze took her in with such thoroughly possessive leisure that all her animosity for him misted away.

"I thought a chauffeur was picking me up."

He unfolded his hands and stepped forward, a smile tugging at his lips. "Ah…but I wanted a few private minutes with you. I caught your speech at the Women CEOs Summit. It was refreshing and bold."

The genuine admiration in his voice... He took the fight out of her far too easily. She licked her lips and said, "Thanks," in an uptight, frosty voice.

Grinning, he neared her. Not quite caging her against the car. But close enough for the fresh, soapy scent of him to assault her every sense. "I never thought about the perils of marrying a woman who's a powerhouse in her own right. Charity galas, and runway shows and photoshoots... I feel quite the poor neglected husband."

A thick, damp lock of hair fell on his forehead and she pushed at it instinctively. The tips of her breasts grazed his bicep and she felt the soft hiss of his breath. "You're not the poor anything, V," she added. Not in the throaty way she'd intended but more like a whisper.

He stepped back, removing that easy intimacy. And his gaze swept over her in an approving survey that spawned warmth.

For all the years she'd spent with makeup artists, Alex preferred simple, easy looks.

The white sleeveless silk blouse draped around her torso was not loose, not figure hugging, but bared a strip of her belly. The inner layer of the skirt ended several inches above her knees, while the outer sheer silky hem fell all the way to her toes, caressing her legs every time she moved.

She'd added diamond studs at her ears and a thin gold chain with a tiny pendant for her jewelry. Her unruly hair, she'd subdued into a French braid while it was still wet.

"You look…different," he added finally.

"Bad different?" she asked, over the loud thudding of her heart.

"Enchanting different," came his quick reply, accompanied by a grin that threatened to take her out at the knees. "You look striking on the runway but I like this version of you more."

"The *not strutting in only three triangles of clothing* version?" she said, cocking her eyebrow.

His laughter dug deep grooves at the sides of his mouth. His gray gaze shone like liquid metal. "That too. But it's not just that. You look real. Like the woman I met in Bali that first night."

Warmth crawled up her neck and she stared, tongue-tied.

Seducing her like this was a game to him. Surrender, his prize.

His thumb traced the dark smudges under her eyes that she hadn't been able to cover up as well as her makeup artist. "However, you look tired." Low and tender, his voice snaked itself around her. "Anna told me your calendar looks impossible."

She tilted her chin up, dislodging his fingers from her skin. "Your assistant should keep her opinions to herself."

This time, he came closer, caging her against the car. Fading sunlight caressed the planes of his face, much like she wanted to. "You're pushing yourself too hard. I don't need Anna to point that out to me."

"This is the pace of my life, V. I want to clear out my calendar and be available for any situation with Charlie."

"You can't run away from your grief, *cara*. Nor can you wrap up six months' worth of work in two. You need to take better—"

"I've been taking care of myself for as long as I can remember. No one else did it for me."

He raised his palms in surrender. "I'm showing concern, *bella*. Not condescension."

The fight went out of her. It wasn't as if the latest designer she was modeling for hadn't muttered about Alex's dress for his show needing to be altered because she'd lost weight. She sighed. "I haven't been sleeping well."

"Missing me in bed?"

"It's not my fault you refuse to stay here at the villa. Neither Leo nor Massimo have any objection to it. You can get to know your br—" he went from warmth to frost in a matter of seconds and Alex took a long breath "—the men you hate, a little better."

A smile broke the stiffness of his upper lip. "You really think you're very clever, *si*?"

"I've no idea what you mean."

"You think putting me under the same roof as Massimo and Leonardo will change my mind?"

"I told you… I have easy access to everything from the villa. I have my design room set up the way I need. Why can't you just move into the villa? Or are you afraid of living under the same room as the men you've loathed for most of your life in case you discover you actually like them?

"As for missing you in bed—" she licked her lips and his gaze got hotter, hungrier "—did you see the ad I did for that sex toy company?"

He grunted and flushed slightly. And it was her turn to laugh.

It wasn't easy to pose as a smitten couple to the world, day in, day out.

Charity galas and fundraisers, cocktail parties, being near each other, the intimate looks and touches, the rush of being near him, of feeling the lean length of him at her back and then ending the evenings abruptly, and not in the pleasurable way they could, was taking a toll on her.

It wasn't so much the sex that Alex wanted—which she absolutely did—but the connection that had come with it. Before and after. The intense high of being seen by a person who really mattered to her. Of being wanted for who she was.

She desperately wanted to find that connection again with him—especially amidst the rubble of their relationship right now. She was terrified that

Greta might be right—it had been unbelievably good sex and nothing more.

Even when they'd been hidden away from the world, it had been she who'd done the chasing. It had been she who'd been desperate to be with him, she who'd wanted their relationship to deepen.

For a man who rarely betrayed his emotions, he had been a revelation in bed. The more she gave, the more he'd demanded of her. Until she'd given him all she had—her heart and soul. Believed that he'd needed her just as she'd needed him.

For all his renewed commitment to their marriage, she wondered at his self-control. Thought again about the original reason he'd married her.

Had he thought she'd be so much putty in his hands as to betray her family? Or had she simply been something to steal away from Greta?

But now that she was getting to know him a little more, now that she understood what drove his actions, that didn't fit with the other pieces of the puzzle.

For all the incredible arrogance of the man, there was no way he could have thought she'd be an asset to him in any way. Then why?

"*Si.* I saw the magazine spread you were kind enough to send me. You nailed the sexy, confident, contemporary woman perfectly."

"Didn't I?" Alex said, a tingly thrill electrifying her all over.

It had been the most fun she'd had in a while. And of course, sending the spread to Vincenzo— her naked limbs peeking out from under a cloud of white sheets with the pink vibrator lying next to her, had been the most fun part of it all. "Anyway, they sent me one as a complimentary gift. Technology is so marvelous, isn't it? It was brilliantly built—steel cloaked in velvet."

"Is there a point to this story?" His jaw tight, the words were gritted out.

"You said I needed stress relief, remember? So the other night, I couldn't sleep and there it was, in its cute pink package. I unpacked it and got back into bed and…"

"And?" he growled as she paused.

"This was my first time using one, you see and—"

In the blink of a breath, he folded his body against hers, one firm hand pulling her arms above her. His breath feathered over her cheeks, his nose rubbing against the tender skin on the inside of one bicep. "You play dirty, *cara*." He whispered the words against the soft flesh of her arm, just above the elbow. His other hand landed unerringly on the narrow strip of skin her outfit bared. Heat from his fingers seared her. "Am I allowed to? Am I allowed to use all the…weapons at my disposal?"

She leaned into his chest, the sides of her breasts pressed against his hard chest. "You already play dirty, V. You use everything you do with me for your PR. Nothing is real anymore."

"What—?"

She meant to back off and miscalculated, their legs tangling instead. Her hip hit the rock-hard slab of his abdomen, her thigh rubbing against his groin. His reaction was instant.

"Oh..." Alex whispered, incapable of rational thought. Her mouth was dry. Punch-drunk on need as she settled her body—chest to thighs, against him.

His fingers dug into her hips as he held her like that, his erection rocking into the notch of her sex. "You think I don't miss you in my bed? You think I was not driven to mindless lust when I saw the magazine spread? You think I didn't take myself in my hand while thinking of you like some rabid fan even though you already belong to me?"

Awareness was a cage around them, the slip and slide of their bodies, the settling of his hard muscles and her softer ones into a familiar groove, begging for that instinctive rhythm to begin...

Hands tight around her, he rocked his hips into her. Their combined moans rent the quiet evening air.

Alex shivered, her skin too tight to contain her. "Please, V…"

"Please what, *bella*?" He licked the sensitive skin at the crook of her neck. And she rubbed her thighs together, desperate for friction there. "Shall I make you climax here, against the car in full view of the villa? Do I win this round then?"

Her own fingers pulling at his hair, Alex buried her face in his throat. "Sometimes, I wish I had never met you on that island. I wish…"

His fingers gentled on her back, as if she hadn't just damned their entire relationship. "I would love to give you what you want. What both of us want. But whom shall you hate more tomorrow morning? Me or yourself?"

Alex drew air in as if her lungs were starved. He was right. This was a dangerous game she was playing. One she might very well lose. "Let me go," she whispered, because it wasn't in her to walk away from him.

He released her slowly, a perfect gentleman. Not betraying by the flicker of an eyelid that he had indeed won this round.

The car pulled away from the villa. For long, silent minutes, Alex lost herself in the spectacular views of the high alpine peaks and the shimmering lake.

His long fingers drew her attention to the steering wheel. The simple but expensive gold band she'd purchased at an exclusive jewelry shop in Bali glinted in the darkness of the interior.

She felt his assessing gaze on her and looked away.

"Do you want to start over and tell me what has you in such a mood?"

"I'm fine."

"No, you're not. As usual, I lost my head when I saw you. Looking like a morsel I wanted to inhale. You were already angry about something."

His perceptiveness didn't surprise her. "This was my only free evening in two weeks. I don't appreciate your personal assistant adding events to my calendar without consulting me first," she said when she finally had a measure of composure. "I need more than—'Important Dinner with Mr. Cavalli—Casual Dress' a few hours before I'm supposed to show up."

"It's easier for Anna to coordinate our mad schedules than constantly talking to your assistant."

Alex didn't miss his obvious affection for the paragon Anna.

The quaint village of Bellagio welcomed them with its narrow, cobblestoned streets and charming alleyways, the Aventador roaring through. "Who's this VIP we're meeting anyway? Another backstabbing board member of BFI who wants more of its profits? Another man who has some kind of vendetta against Leo and Massimo?"

"We're meeting an old friend of mine. Antonio is…he's very dear to me. And despite my many warnings, he and some other friends have arranged a surprise party for us in his house, to celebrate our marriage. I would appreciate it if you can put aside our differences for a few hours and treat him with the respect he deserves."

His gruff request took Alex by surprise. "I'll act as if you were my sun and moon. As if you were the answer to my every romantic fantasy."

"Alessandra, this is important to me." His sigh rattled in the silence. "I wanted to give both Antonio and you a chance to meet outside of what will definitely become a media circus once I take over BFI. I don't want us talking about how you abandoned our marriage on our honeymoon or how you only returned to make a deal with me for your brother's sake. Antonio's a very traditional man."

"Shall we also not talk about how you kept your biggest ambition a secret from me? And how—"

"Antonio knows my background. My goal all these years. All the things I've done."

All the things he'd done…

Suddenly, Alex felt as if she was being given a key to unlock this man. To understand him better. To find some way to stop him. To figure out if her first instinct about their marriage had been right, that there was something to salvage from this mess.

Vincenzo stopped the car near the lakefront. A row of pretty, colorful houses opened up the narrow winding street. When Alex reached for the door, he swung an arm across her torso toward the handle, locking her in place. The corded strength of his forearm pressed between her breasts, sending pulses of awareness jerking through her.

The sun had set during their drive and the interior of the car was faintly lit.

"We have been on display for three whole weeks now, ever since the news broke. I thought a quiet night would do us some good. There's no pressure to be in the spotlight tonight."

"I would like advance notice about these things. Especially if I'm to appear in good humor."

"I asked you for one evening, Alessandra, for an important thing."

"It would be nice if things that were important to me were valued just as equally by you."

"*Cristo!* What the hell's bothering you?"

"There are certain things I can't forgive, Vincenzo. I just can't."

"Yes, *cara*. And we're both constantly testing those certain limits, aren't we?"

"Everything you do with me is for the media—I understand that. Your damned PR team used that kiss at the nightclub to its full extent.

To put a romantic spin on the whole thing. Used it to cloud the very real threat you pose to Leo and Massimo."

"This whole charade was *your* plan. Do you think that I forget for one moment that you came back to me for your own damned reasons, however noble they are? That not for a single hour will you forget your ties to that blasted family? You're the one who wanted to show the world that you're settling down into a life of domesticity and stability, *bella*."

"Yes. And it's enough that we're parading ourselves in front of this media circus. That we pretend as if we can't keep our hands off each other. But some things are not for public consumption. Some things are not..."

"What on earth are you talking about?"

"The picture of our wedding. The only one we have. The one I asked that passing local to click. Neither your PR team nor your wonderful assistant asked me for permission before they released that picture to the press."

His disbelief showed in the jerk of his head. "Alessandra—"

"You entered this marriage for God knows what reasons of your own. I have tried to put those behind me. I've convinced myself that what I want doesn't matter anymore. That this is all for Charlie. I have tucked away my foolish hopes.

"But that picture...it's precious to me. That

moment was real, at least it was to me. In fact, it was the most real moment of my life, and you used it to manipulate the world.

"You stole it from me."

"You stole it from me."

Alessandra's words echoed inside Vincenzo's head as he made the rounds on the beautiful, moonlit terrace of Antonio's small house and greeted acquaintances and friends he hadn't seen in a long time. Even in the dark of the car's interior, he'd seen the glint of hurt in those beautiful eyes. The catch in her words.

Reminding him that beneath the fiery woman who'd strutted so confidently across the runway, beneath the woman that challenged him at every step, beneath the mantle of responsibility she'd put on for her half brother, his wife was vulnerable.

To him, his actions, his words.

And that very quality he'd wanted to see in her sat uncomfortably in his chest. Weighting him down.

It made him want to banish the hurt from her eyes. Made him want to protect her from anything in the world that could cause her pain. Including him.

Dio santo! If that wasn't messed up, he didn't know what was.

He turned to look at the tall, elegant figure

of his wife, standing amidst a group of people, a soft smile playing around her lips. The same lips that had whispered such provocative words in his ear, pushing him to the edge of his control.

She was tallest of the group, and the most beautiful, by a wide margin. And yet when one of the teenagers Vincenzo had known for a while, Marco, approached her and said something, she nodded and laughed. Boxing, they were talking about boxing, he knew.

She handed off her wineglass to someone else, got into position with an animated smile and showed Marco her mean right hook. The toned curve of her arm, the flash of thigh as she pulled the inner skirt up to stretch her legs into a fighting stance, the utter joy in her eyes as she ducked Marco's left fist... She looked incredibly sexy.

He could see the people he worked with reassess their opinion of her. Could sense their shock as they realized there was so much more to Alessandra than her looks.

"She's not what I expected from you," Antonio said, handing Vincenzo a glass of the bubbly champagne that they had been toasted with earlier.

Vincenzo looked at the man who had given him a sense of purpose when he'd been lost. Not just moral support. Antonio had provided seed money when he'd been starting out. He'd helped Vincenzo go from strength to strength. He owed everything he had to the older man. But… Some things, Vincenzo considered private. Off-limits. Even to Antonio.

It was the most real moment of my life.

Suddenly, he understood what Alessandra meant by that, and regret filled him.

He took a sip of his champagne. Laughter and shouts surrounded him as Alessandra's fist gently connected with another youth's angular chin. "What did you expect?"

Antonio shrugged, his weathered face splitting into a smile that didn't really reach his eyes. "An international supermodel, Vincenzo! Parties, and designer dresses and the high life…all sparkle and no substance."

Vincenzo didn't like hearing Alessandra reduced to being some one-dimensional bimbo. "Alessandra's more than just a supermodel. Give her a chance, Antonio."

"All of us fall victim to stereotyping, *si*?" The older man laughed at his own joke. "Hearing that you married is shocking in itself. You never even hinted at wanting to settle down in all these years."

"No, it was never on my mind."

"If I had known, I might have suggested a better alternative," Antonio said, his gray head nodding in another direction. Vincenzo turned and saw his assistant Anna, standing stiffly to one side, a frosty smile fixed in place. What the hell did Antonio mean by that? "You need a strong, steady woman who can stand by you like a rock, Vincenzo. Who knows her place in your life. Not this…frothy creature from some fantasyland."

"She's my wife, Antonio. And I never gave Anna the idea that she meant anything more to me."

"After all, you're a man too," Antonio added with a shrug. His gaze shifted back to Alessandra, who was now talking to Anna. "Ah…so the woman is as irresistible as she looks, then, *si*?"

Vincenzo shrugged. Even with Antonio, he didn't want to admit to the complete truth.

Which was that he had completely lost his mind over Alessandra. Continued to, in fact. Her loyalty to the Brunettis amazed him. Her determination to do right by her half brother resonated deep inside him. Her vulnerability when it came to himself… Shook him. At a level he hadn't thought possible.

"Her Brunetti connection is an unnecessary headache you don't need right now. A distraction from your true purpose," the older man insisted.

"It is a headache. She—" Vincenzo swallowed the word *hates* "—does not like what I intend to do to them. In fact, she's waging a quiet campaign to shift me from my plans, I believe."

The warm glint disappeared from Antonio's dark eyes. "And? Do you think she will succeed?"

Vincenzo frowned at the quiet question. "You know me better than that, Antonio. She's a small part of my life. An indulgence I allow myself." He didn't say she was fast becoming an obsession he craved. When she looked at him with that vulnerability in her eyes, he wanted to promise her the world. He wanted to promise her anything just to make her smile again. "Alessandra is a prize. A worthy wife for a man building an empire. She's the final reward for all the fights I have won and for the ones I'm still waging."

"And yet you watch her with such hunger in your eyes. As if you don't already own her. As if you want…more."

More… Did he want more from Alessandra? More of what?

Vincenzo refused to betray how accurate Antonio's words were. "Maybe you've forgotten what it is to look at a woman you want, Antonio. I do not deny that she's got a hold over me."

"That bothers me. About how powerful her hold is on you. About how much you will forgive her, how much you will forget in order to please her."

"Speak your mind plainly, Antonio."

"I'm not so old that I do not keep up with the news. She set you back a few steps with that leak about who you really are. The financial world is still wondering where you come from, how you've amassed your fortune and with what intentions. You lost the support of two men who were almost in your pocket. Now you have to begin the hunt anew to find other candidates who will stand against the combined might of Leonardo and Massimo Brunetti."

"My PR team has been doing a lot of damage control since then. But it's not Alessandra who leaked that information."

"And you believe her?" The older man's softly spoken words resonated with doubt and disbelief.

"Yes," Vincenzo replied firmly.

"We've worked far too hard, for far too long to bring the Brunettis down. This marriage of yours could derail everything. Worse, it could—"

"I want to build what I have been denied all my life—a standing in society, a home to return to, a dynasty. What will stand in its place when the past is brought to its knees?" Vincenzo demanded, angry and tired and resentful in a way he'd never felt before. "For the first time in my life, I acted selfishly. It is neither a mistake nor a strategic move."

Did Antonio see him as nothing but a device for vengeance? Was there anything left of him that wasn't a weapon to fuel him toward his goal? This restlessness… He realized it had been growing in him for a while. A small crack that threatened to expand into a yawning void every time he visited his mother.

And then he had met Alessandra.

A breath of fresh air. A woman who had filled his days with laughter and warmth reminded him that he was a man who wanted more. A woman who made him think of the future.

"As long as it doesn't distract you from your mission," added Antonio, his expression implacable. That implacability had once been the backbone that had built Vincenzo's confidence sky-high. Antonio's belief had goaded him to the heights of success and through dark nights of self-doubt. And yet now, it felt like a painful echo from the past he couldn't outrun.

"It does not mean that I've forgotten." He ran a hand through his hair, tension swathing his frame. "I cannot, even if I wished it. Every time I see Mama…" He swallowed and looked away. His wound would never heal. Because every time he saw his mother, it was gouged afresh. "Keep your trust in me, Antonio."

The old man gripped Vincenzo's shoulder. "I do. Maybe this is not a bad move. Maybe you can use your wife to move even faster toward your goal."

Everything in Vincenzo rebelled against the idea. "What do you mean?"

"You and Leonardo Brunetti are in a deadlock now for majority on the BFI board, *si*?"

"*Si.*"

"The matriarch, Greta Brunetti, still holds stock in BFI, doesn't she? If your wife is truly important to her, maybe she could be persuaded to jump ship in your favor."

Shock pulsed through Vincenzo. *"I'll be damned before I let you use me against them,"* Alessandra had vowed.

"You want me to persuade Greta Brunetti to betray her own grandsons if she wants Alessandra's happiness?"

"There must be some substance to your wife's devotion to the old woman and that family. Test that connection. See how far you can push them with it.

"Think of it this way, Vincenzo. The faster you win this war, the faster you break up BFI into parts, the sooner you can settle into a blissful wedded life."

Vincenzo couldn't muster a reply. To use Alessandra and her happiness as a bargaining weapon against Greta Brunetti... The very thought filled him with distaste. What kind of a man would he have become then?

"I'd like to go home now, please. If you're done for the night," Alessandra whispered with a polite smile pasted on her mouth the moment Vincenzo reached her.

"That picture of us on the morning of our wedding...leaking it to the press... I never gave a direct, specific instruction to do that." He pressed his fingers to her mouth when she'd have protested. "Hear me out, please, Alessandra.

"And before you shred my team into pieces, they only followed my order—to a T—that they improve my image in the media.

"So, yes, the ultimate responsibility is mine, but it was a thoughtless, general action rather than a deliberate, strategic one to hurt you, or to lessen the significance of that day for you."

Her beautiful brown gaze mirrored her disbelief and hurt.

Vincenzo took her fingers in his and pressed. A harsh exhale left him when she didn't pull away. "I should have realized it was so important to you. I should have—"

"It doesn't matter."

"*Si!* It does matter. What you think of all this, it does matter." He'd been about to say *What you think of me*, but held it back, "I'm beginning to understand how much what I did hurt you. But my intentions for you, for this marriage have always been the same. From the beginning."

She held his gaze, as if she could hold him to his word like that. As if she could see into his heart.

"Just promise me that you won't use me in this battle of yours," she said.

"I won't. I have already said our marriage will stand outside of it. Come now, Princess. Dance with me."

She said nothing. Didn't move.

"It's a beautiful night. And I want to dance with my beautiful wife. I want to show all the men salivating over you that you're mine. Only mine."

Vincenzo waited. For all of Antonio's disapproval, he knew in his heart that she was the one he wanted when he finally reached the end of all this. She was the one who had birthed the future he hadn't even realized could be his.

He left his hand outstretched. Finally, with a soft sigh, she came to him. And everything else ceased to exist for Vincenzo. The crowd around them, the soft music, the moonlight, everything became secondary to the sensation of having Alessandra in his arms.

She was like liquid silk poured over taut, warm limbs, her face hidden in the curve of his shoulder. Her fingers a brand on the nape of his neck. Her breaths a soft whisper against his skin. For long minutes, they just moved to the music, their bodies easily swaying in a matching rhythm.

"You stole it from me."

"Have you forgiven me yet?" he whispered. "For making that picture public."

"You're who you are." The defeat in those words slayed him.

"I...there was something between us on the island, *si*. But I think, in the real world, we've broken that trust. Both of us."

She lifted her head and stared straight into his eyes. And nodded slowly. She pulled away from him and leaned against the balcony. The chitchat around them carried on, but everyone was giving them a wide berth.

She looked around, her gaze thoughtful. "All these people...they worship the ground you walk on."

"That's a bit dramatic."

She shook her head. "I don't think so."

"They have known me for a long time, *si*. When I had nothing to my name, when I was nothing but a boy with big dreams. Even from a young age, I had a way with numbers. The stock market was an easy pattern for me to predict."

"Like Massimo is brilliant with computers," she interjected.

He let it go. "Antonio saw my talent and nurtured it. When I started playing the market, these people trusted me with their savings. When I started my investment firm, they were my first clients. They trusted me to do right by them. Now that I have a million times more, I try to remember them. I try to give it back."

"I'm glad you were not all alone. But it's still not family."

He shrugged.

"She's in love with you, you know."

His head jerked to her. "What the hell are you talking about?"

She wrapped her arms around herself, her wide mouth pinched. "Your assistant, Anna. It's obvious. She thinks...they all think I'm a back-stabbing witch who doesn't deserve you."

"What?"

"Were the two of you ever together?"

Vincenzo blew out a breath, looking out at Alessandra and then back toward a small group where Anna stood talking.

Antonio's remark had suddenly made him see Anna's frosty reception toward Alessandra clearly. "A long time ago. Years before I met you. And it was only ever a brief fling that I put a stop to as soon as we started working together."

"And yet she had hopes that it would eventually be rekindled."

He didn't discount the truth of it now he understood. "Then it is my fault for not making myself clear to her. I never even realized until... Alessandra, I never led Anna on."

"I believe you." Said with such simplicity that he stared at her, stunned. "She told me that you have had an architect draw up plans for the Brunetti Villa. That you intend to pull it down and build something else in its place. That you mean to take over BFI by the bicentennial celebrations."

Shock pounded through him. "Anna would never be so unprofessional as to betray my plans."

"How else do you think I know about them?

She hates my guts, because she thinks I stole her man, and she wants me to leave you. They couldn't be more shocked if you had suddenly taken up farming, V." Her gaze turned thoughtful. "Apparently, you went full on rogue in this operation by marrying me."

"My life is not a democracy for them to vote on."

A frown tied her brows. "It sure sounds like it is."

"You're my wife, Alessandra. If Anna can't realize how important that is, she will have to be let go. I'm sorry she made you uncomfortable tonight."

"How about you're sorry for all the things you hide from me? How about you're sorry that you ever conceived those plans in the first place?"

"Again, they were in place long before I met you. These people have been in my life for many years while you…"

"While I what, V?"

"While you flit in and out of it. While you run away from me the moment the fantasy falls apart."

"And if I do stay in this marriage? When you take over BFI and break it down into parts, when you raze that villa to the ground and build a new one in its stead, is that where you expect me to live?

"Is that where we're supposed to start our new family? Our new life?"

"Si."

"Leo and Massimo will never give up their home."

"We shall see about that."

"Love cannot grow where there's so much hate, V."

"But I've never asked you for love," he bit out, and she flinched. A wet sheen coated her eyes and Vincenzo wanted to believe it was caused by the suddenly cold breeze. "Is that why you married me, *bella*? Because you fancied yourself in love with me?" Neither could he take the bitter edge out of his words.

It was high time they discussed their expectations. High time he set the record straight that he wasn't going to change his mind about his course of action just because she was in his life. "Was it love that made you run at the first hurdle? That made you abandon our marriage when it had barely started?

"That makes you imagine I should give up things I've set into motion years before I met you?"

He reached for her and set his hands on her shoulders. She stiffened but didn't push him away, those gorgeous brown eyes of hers drilling into him. "Love is for fools who don't realize how it can turn to poison in a minute. It pushed Anna into jeopardizing her position with me.

"It drove my mother into believing falsely

sweet promises from a monster and breaking the heart of a simple man who respected her and admired her."

"Antonio?"

"*Si*. And when he demanded Silvio Brunetti do right by her, when he dared take him on, Brunetti crushed Antonio, as if he were an ant. He came for his business, for his family. He ruined everything Antonio had and anyone who dared helped him."

She looked around the empty terrace, her eyes widening. Comprehension twisted her features into horror. "All these people you've collected, you've surrounded yourself with…they are all—"

"They've all been harmed one way or the other by the mighty Brunetti family, *si*."

"By Silvio Brunetti," she amended. "Not by Leo and Massimo." She stepped back from him, her mouth compressed. He'd never seen her look more defeated. "They're all equally invested in the path of destruction they want you to take. Even if you wanted to walk away from it now, they won't let you. That explains their chilly attitude toward me. They think I will turn your head."

"You won't," he reiterated so forcefully that she flinched.

"Well, that's put me in my place," she added with an empty laugh. "But in the end, you'll be the only one who pays the price, V. Not them.

You'll be the one who stands on the ashes of your family's happiness, ruining any chance of a relationship with them."

"My family? If you think even for a moment that I will ever consider Leo and Massimo to be my family at the end of all this, that somehow we will become brothers in truth…then you're even more naive than I'd ever thought.

"They are not my family. They were not there for me when I struggled to fill my belly. When I saw Mama become a shadow of herself. When I had no money to pay for treatment for her."

"But you—"

"This is not your fight, *cara*. Let it go."

"And if this fight ends up hurting us, V? If it ruins any chance of happiness that we might have had?"

He stared into her eyes, the answer jolting out of him. Somehow, somewhere along the way, Alessandra had gotten under his skin. Had begun to matter to him more and more.

But only so much. It could only ever be so much that he could give her. Only so much he could feel. He didn't know how to be vulnerable. To remove the very defenses he'd put up for sheer survival.

He couldn't give voice to that yes that whispered in his chest. Couldn't let himself become so caught up in her that he forgot all the years of loneliness and fear and pain. Forgot what he'd set out to do. To prove.

To the world. And to himself.

"Whether my actions hurt you is not in my hands, Alessandra. It's in yours. In the end, we all have to make choices.

"Whether you want this marriage only for Charlie's sake or for yourself, you have to decide. You need to decide how much of this is just a deal and how much is real.

"Because for me, nothing has changed. Not since I slipped that ring on your finger."

The stricken look in her eyes told him she more than got the message. And as much as it bothered him to leave her like that, he walked away.

A strange tension gripped him but he refused to give it a name. He could have used the attraction between them, the constant tug of awareness to nudge her over into acceptance. But Vincenzo needed her to come to him. Needed her to choose him.

Like he wanted nothing else in his life.

He didn't examine the urge, didn't rationalize it. It was just there.

And yet as he joined Antonio and the others— people who had always been on his side, people who looked at him with respect and admiration, people who had looked to him to solve the injustices done them—for the first time in his life he felt as though he didn't fit in with them either.

CHAPTER SEVEN

IT WAS THE last scene Alex had ever imagined she'd come home to when she returned to the Brunetti villa the following Friday evening after an exhausting, weeklong trip to New York to visit Charlie.

Leo, Massimo and Greta were dining al fresco on the terrace, making the most of a beautiful late September evening. But the magnificent view couldn't hold Alex's attention.

Seated by Massimo, his arrogant head jerking up at her as she walked up the last step, was Vincenzo.

His gaze held hers over the length of the terrace, awareness stretching between them, holding her captive. For a few seconds, Alessandra forgot her exhaustion, the fresh grief that had been raked up the past week, the uncertainty of where all this would end.

When she looked at Vincenzo, she forgot everything but him.

"How is your brother, Alessandra?" His question, in a dry tone, pulled Alex out of her reverie.

Alex blinked, feeing heat climb up her cheeks. "He's okay. I wish he cried a little more though, or screamed or something. He's far too self-contained for a seven-year-old boy."

"But then boys are often taught that it's a weakness to cry," Massimo added with a bitterness that made her heart ache.

Alex saw the disbelief in Vincenzo's eyes.

"Our father verbally abused Massimo, unchallenged, for years." This little nugget was supplied by Leonardo.

His jaw tight, Vincenzo stared at both men. Alex held her breath, waiting for him to rip into these men who had enough courage to own up to their torturous childhoods with the man Vincenzo thought had abandoned him.

But Vincenzo remained silent and with it didn't invalidate the pain of the brothers he considered his enemies.

"Charlie told me one of the boys at school has been bullying him," she said, running a hand through her hair. "I reported it to his teacher and she's looking into it. However, I also taught him how to sucker punch the bully if he ever bothered him again."

All three men simultaneously cheered on that suggestion, and the tension broke.

"Come, sit down, *bella*. Unless you're planning on leaving again," Vincenzo drawled, an edge of censure in his tone. He looked up at her, and she had that feeling of being consumed by his gaze. Only it wasn't just desire. It was more. "Soon, you're going to run out of places to hide."

Heat washed over her face, but Alex took the chair he pulled out for her. "I had my mother's affairs to take care of in New York. Her husband's estate is huge. Not to mention the fact that Charlie was missing me. I did text you that I was leaving."

"Ah, yes, so you did. Five minutes before take-off."

She refused to let him put her in the wrong this time. "What would you have done if I had told you any earlier? You're so busy spinning your webs around people. It's hard enough that I can't even give Charlie a specific date yet as to when he can join me."

"Maybe I would have joined you in going to New York, Alessandra. Did you think of that?"

Alex jerked her gaze to his. "Why?"

"For the simple fact that you're going through a lot in your life right now and I wanted to be there to support you? For the logical fact that it would have been sensible to present a united front to Charlie's extended family and the lawyers?

"To reassure Charlie himself that I'm just

as invested in his well-being as you are? I'm a stranger to him, after all."

Shame streaked bright color across Alex's face, and she struggled to hold his gaze. He was right. It was the whole point of their deal, after all. And yet, all she'd wanted was a reprieve.

From the emotional turmoil he plunged her into with one look, one touch, one kiss.

From the trust he demanded she give him without having earned it.

The more she learned about him, the more complex he turned out to be. This whole thing had never been simply about revenge, or ambition, or wanting power for himself. Not the man who'd helped so many, who had such a strong moral compass.

Her first instinct that he was a man worthy of knowing had been right.

The more she wanted to remain detached, the more she felt lured in. Before, she'd been afraid of the harm he would cause Leo and Massimo and Greta, but now she was beginning to worry about him.

About the bitterness she'd seen in his eyes when he spoke of his mother. About what would be left of him when all this was done. About the crushing emptiness that would come no matter his material success if there was no one to share it with.

She rubbed the pads of her fingers over her

tired eyes. "I'm sorry. You were right. I… I didn't think of all those eminently sensible reasons."

He clutched her fingers on the table and squeezed. "You're still fighting this, *bella.*"

She nodded and pulled her fingers away. Three gazes watched them with varied levels of interest.

"What finally convinced you to come here to the villa?" she asked him, reaching for a glass of wine.

"I was getting bored of sleeping alone," he said bluntly.

Greta's fork clattered onto the plate.

"I invited him," Leo said into the awkward silence. "Neha reminded me that in all this…you're the one caught in the middle.

"So I will tell you again, Alex, and in front of him, this time.

"Neither Massimo nor I expect you to fight for us. But if you need an out from this marriage, if for any reason you want to be done with it, we'll throw everything we have behind you."

The absolute fury in Vincenzo's eyes in contrast to the stillness that came over him had Alex drawing in a sharp breath.

"Telling my wife that you'll help her walk away from me, in front of me, is surely a fool's play, Leonardo." The very smoothness of his words raised the hairs on her neck. "Like waving a red flag in front of a bull. Especially after all the work poor Alessandra has been putting in to persuade me to rethink your ruin."

Leo didn't even bat an eyelid. "No threat of ruin will make me forget my priorities, Cavalli. You think you had it hard? You didn't have our father filling your head with poison when you barely knew right and wrong. You didn't have to unlearn toxic truths about why your own mother would desert you.

"I had to protect my family, and myself, from him, when I was barely a man. And Alex has been a part of this family for a long time."

Again, Vincenzo stayed silent.

Alex chewed her salad, feeling a spark of hope for the first time in weeks, while Leo and Massimo started casually chatting about the upcoming bicentennial celebrations of BFI. The preparations were already in full force.

She had told neither Leo nor Massimo about Vincenzo's plans for the villa or BFI. God, she hated being the bearer of bad news. Especially when there was nothing she could do to help them. Fortunately, both of them had been out of town when she'd returned that night, still reeling under the impact of all she'd learned.

"Did you clear your calendar for the celebration, Alex?" Massimo asked. "There will be journalists, of course. But also, a photographer for the family's photoshoot for the feature they're doing on BFI's history."

"I'll sit that one out if you don't mind," she replied.

Vincenzo covered her hand on the table, his gaze filled with a wicked humor. "Of course, she will come. We will both be here to celebrate the success of such a long-standing venerable institution as BFI. Especially on such a momentous day."

If Greta heard the resounding mockery in his words, she didn't let it show. Slowly, she pushed her chair back, and stood. She pressed one hand into Alex's shoulder and then walked away. Without a word.

The stoop of Greta's proud shoulders made a lump settle in Alex's throat. Greta's past actions and Alex's present sat like painful, snarly knots in their relationship. She hadn't realized how much Greta's implacable but quiet presence in her life meant to her. Until Alex had lost it.

Massimo and Leo followed Greta.

The moment it was just them, Alex turned on Vincenzo.

To find him frowning, a thoughtful tilt to his mouth.

"What are you doing here at the villa? What new game are you up to?" she demanded.

"Following your dictates," Vincenzo replied silkily, sitting back in his chair.

Alex slammed her wineglass down, hard

enough for it to slosh over her fingers. "Please, V. No more games."

"I hate living like a bachelor in hotels when I have a perfectly nice wife here at the villa. I realized you were right all along."

"You mean you realized you can torment Greta in her own home?"

"Asking me to behave as if I finally found my long-lost grandmother is a bit much, even for you, *bella*."

Why had she thought bringing Vincenzo face-to-face with the Brunettis would be a good idea? Already, her head was pounding. "If you think you're going to wear her down into regretting her actions, you'll wait forever. To her, the past is done, V. She had to deal with the consequences of every selfish, vile act Silvio perpetrated, and that has turned her into stone."

"Consequences that became the crumbling foundation of my life."

"I'm not asking you to forgive her."

"*Bene*. Because I hate disappointing you."

"Do you really? Is this all anything other than a game to you?" she demanded.

She'd had enough. It felt as if she was still dreaming, amidst the fitful sleep she'd caught on the flight back to Milan. Wondering if all the pieces would ever come together. Wondering if she would always feel ripped apart by conflicting loyalties.

She pushed away her chair, every inch of her vibrating with an internal fight she couldn't win. "I'm out of here."

"Alessandra—"

"I have to get ready. There's a designer launch in Milan. I have to show my face." Although the thought of being in front of cameras right now made her want to throw up.

Vincenzo followed her down the steps. "I contacted your agent and got you out of it."

Alex stilled. "What? That's… How dare you?"

"Alessandra, you look like you'll collapse if someone blows hard enough."

"And whose fault is that? I just spent an entire week going through my mother's things. Sorting what to keep and what to give away. For Charlie. Her entire life…in boxes, V. Then I came back to this. I know why you can't forgive Greta for what she did to you and your mother. Even I can't. But…have you thought for one minute that I might actually need you? That I might want to lean on you?"

"Of course, yes."

"I'm so foolish. I can't believe I actually thought it would be a good idea for you to be here. You're right. I'm pathetic and—"

His arms enveloped her so tightly that Alex was forced to stop shivering. "Shh…*tesoro*. Shh…breathe, Alessandra."

"Sometimes, I feel so alone. It doesn't matter

what I do, or where I run. In the end, I'm always terrifyingly alone."

"Look at me, *bella*. Concentrate on me."

Alex looked up and the panic that had been closing in on her receded. She focused on her reflection in the gray of his eyes. Breathed in until that fresh, crisp scent of him was an anchor in her blood. Let herself drown in the warmth his body gave off.

A tear rolled down her cheek and he held her gently. As if she was the most precious thing in his life. "You're not alone, Alessandra. I'm here. *Mi dispiace...* I'm sorry, you were right. I forget how much you've been through."

In that moment, he was the haven she'd been looking for all her life. He was the prince she'd always wanted. He held her heart in the palm of his hand.

And Alex wanted nothing more than to sink into his strong body. Nothing more than to share the grief that choked her sometimes. Nothing more than to give herself over to him.

But the girl who'd been seen by her own mother as a punishment, the girl who'd always wondered what she'd done wrong, the girl whose heart had been seriously dented over the last few months, reared its head. Bringing rationality along.

She looked up into those magnetic eyes, forcing herself to break the spell. "Why?"

"Why what?"

"Why do you act as if this marriage is so important to you?"

His curse rang around in the garden. "Because it is." He ran a hand through his hair and she realized, even he didn't know why. "It just is." But the conviction she wanted was there. In his gaze. In the set of his mouth.

"Why?" she pushed, instinctively realizing they were standing on the cusp of something vital.

"Because you made me see a future for myself. All my life, I had no plans beyond the destruction of the Brunettis. I came to Bali because I had been so curious about you, about your role within the family. But when I got there, when we met, it… I have never acted like this with a woman before. There's no precedent for my actions."

A burst of air burned her lungs as Alex took in a deep breath. All around her, fragrance filled the air. The sounds and scents of life itself underscoring the hope flickering in her chest.

He was right. She couldn't do justice to anyone this way, sitting on the fence in the middle of everyone. She had to choose. She wanted to choose him. She wanted to bridge this gap between them. She wanted to hope that everything would turn out for the best.

"You really want to spend time with me?"

"I've barely seen you for more than a few

hours since the wedding. Either you're finishing off a contract, or saving *them* from me, or showing up for Charlie on the other side of the world." His thumb traced the dark circles under her eyes. "I would feel quite the neglected husband if I didn't see that you're neglecting yourself too."

She shrugged. But she couldn't conjure the energy to dislodge his hands. No, she didn't want to dislodge them. She was tired of fighting. She wanted to be held. By him. It was an ache in her belly, this want. "We both have busy lifestyles."

"I miss you, *bella*. That's why I moved in here. I miss—" he swallowed, his eyes glinting with desire and awareness, slamming into Alex like a bulldozer "—spending time with you."

She snorted, a lightness filling her despite the emotional roller coaster of the last week. It was hard not to be moved by the raw need in those eyes. "You mean you miss sex?"

"Si." He ran a hand through his hair. "But I miss having sex with *you*."

And just like that, he felled her where she stood with that raw admission, with that naked hunger he made no attempt to hide in his eyes.

Electricity arced between them, and she found herself swaying toward him. Every cell in her begging to give in.

His palm kneaded her hip with gentle pressure, his powerful thighs teasing sinuously against her own. "Stop running away, Alex," he whispered in her ear.

He touched his mouth to the line of her jaw, his breath a caress against her skin. Heart beating a thousand to the minute, Alex leaned into him. Those soft lips drew a lightning path down her cheek until they reached the corner of her mouth. And stilled. A meteor dropping on them couldn't have moved her then.

"Maybe catch up on your sleep first, *bella.*

"Because we have a lot to make up for."

Vincenzo closed the door of Alessandra's bedroom softly behind him. The gaunt set of her face—*maledizione*, she looked like stretched glass—haunted him as he walked through the long corridor toward the room he had set up as a temporary study.

Lust he understood. She was gorgeous and more than matched his appetite in bed.

But this tenderness when he'd found her fast asleep on top of the bedcovers, still in the sweats and old T-shirt she'd worn this evening, dark shadows under her eyes—this he didn't understand.

He stayed inattentive all through the conference call with Massimo and BFI's CFO, two of the most dynamic board members of BFI, both Leo's recruits.

Frustration raked through him as the call

ended. The second man left while Massimo closed his laptop with a hard thud that spoke all too loud.

"You won't find anything against him," Massimo said calmly.

"What?" Vincenzo spat out, his mind all too focused on his wife. And the very real grief he'd glimpsed in her eyes earlier that evening. Grief for her mother that she still refused to share with him.

"You won't find any dirt on Leo. Or me, for that matter."

Vincenzo looked back at the younger man he was unwillingly coming to more than respect. "Look, Massimo—"

"Don't insult my intelligence, Cavalli. You've been like a rabid dog these past few weeks trying to find ammunition against Leo.

"The men who are hungrily following in your wake to oust him…those are the kind of men Leo took on in the first place in his fight to turn BFI around. Who didn't agree with him when he instituted an ethics committee, who didn't want to give up even a small share of their profits to clean up the mess Silvio created.

"But then you already know all this."

Massimo picked up his laptop and crossed the room. "For a man who hates the name Brunetti and everything it stands for, you very much act like one, Cavalli."

The air left his lungs as if he'd been gut punched. "Don't you dare—"

"No? It's a Brunetti trait to destroy the very people who might save us.

"Didn't you realize that in all the research you did on us? Didn't Natalie tell you I almost lost her because of how screwed up I had been? Isn't that what you're doing to Alex?

"Our father—*si*, our *father*," he emphasized when Vincenzo flinched, "drove away two good women who could have turned him away from his destructive path.

"See this through and you're truly his son. More than Leo and I have ever been."

Massimo's words ate through Vincenzo like acid, eating away at his resolution, corroding his certainty.

Destroy the name Brunetti and everything it entailed in this world. That had been his goal for so long. A number of people were counting on him.

But the Brunettis were men he was coming to see as more than honorable. Despite all his aggressive tactics, there had been no attempt at retaliation from either.

In fact, they had invited him into their home, the very home he wanted to ruin.

All the evidence only pointed to the fact that they cared about what he did to Alessandra. Not to them.

He had started on this path to right a multitude of wrongs, yes. But he never wanted to hurt an innocent in the process. He was beginning to feel like a man caught uncomfortably between his past and present. A man caught between his promises and his own selfishness.

And the woman he'd married so impulsively, who'd looked today as if he was breaking her apart, she was caught in the middle of it all with him.

Alex stood inside the huge BFI office that Leonardo occupied, indecision cleaving her in half. She had a decision to make. Vincenzo had been right. And the fact that she'd turned up here meant a part of her had already made it.

But she couldn't just leave things in limbo anymore. Not after she'd learned about Antonio and all the people who'd been harmed by Silvio Brunetti. Not after finally understanding the burden Vincenzo had been living with for so many years, the burden that fueled his need for justice.

Now she knew what fired him. He was still wrong, but God, she couldn't just walk away from him. She couldn't just sit tight while there was still a chance that she could do something to help him heal.

"Did you mean what you said at the villa yesterday?" she asked the question before the vulnerability she felt swallowed it up. Before she second-guessed herself again.

Leo and Massimo turned as one, Milan's skyline behind them a beautiful blend of orange and
blue. Shock and concern played on their achingly
familiar faces as they took her in.

"Alex? Is everything okay?" Leo asked, coming away from his desk. His tie had been undone,
and his jacket discarded. Alex saw the lines of
worry that had deepened on his face and felt guilt
slam into her yet again. God, he was already worried about Neha and the babies she carried since
her blood pressure was too high. Now she…

"I'm sorry. I shouldn't have come."

Massimo moved like lightning, blocking her
before she could take two steps away. "No, *bella*.
Don't run away."

"Of course I meant every word," Leo said behind her, his words ringing with conviction. He
clasped her shoulder and squeezed. "This is not,
and never was your battle to fight, Alex. You
don't owe us anything."

Alex took a deep breath and turned around.
For as long as she'd known him, Leonardo had
been fair and honorable, determined to be different from the man who'd sired him.

His gaze swept over hers with concern, and he
sighed. "Say what's on your mind, Alex."

"I know you can't forgive Vincenzo for what
he's doing. For everything he's already done. But
I understand his reasons now. For years, he's been
caught up in this, fighting for justice for people

who can't demand it for themselves. And while he's laying the blame at the wrong feet, his reasons are…painfully just. I need you guys to believe me that he's not…a monster. I can't…go on with my marriage if you think that. I just can't. You are both too important to me. You're family."

"And nothing will change that, Alex. We already know he's not a monster, *bella*," Massimo interjected, coming to stand by her. "Even if we forget, Natalie reminds us daily. Any man who willingly helps a lost teenager couldn't be one."

"And will you forgive me if I…stay with him?"

Massimo whistled and Leo sent him a glare. "You don't need forgiveness. Alex, this is your life. Your happiness. Whatever choice you make, we'll still love you." Leo sighed. "As long as he doesn't hurt you."

"He won't," Alex said, not knowing where the words came from. Where the trust came from.

But she'd done enough running in her life, lost enough by not staying and fighting. Her mother was never coming back. And she couldn't bear to lose this chance with Vincenzo too.

When she spoke, her words rang with conviction. "He won't hurt me, Leo. He has reasons for his actions. So many of them. He can't see anything else right now. But there's more to him than this revenge. He's a man worth standing by. And I want to try."

Massimo wrapped his arm around her, as if

he could sense how tightly stretched she was. "We've been preparing for the worst for a long time, *bella*. Before he stepped into your life."

"And even if he takes everything we have built, we'll rebuild again. He's not going to make us destitute, Alex. I hope you have that much trust in us," Leo added archly, and Alex smiled, despite the tears in her eyes.

How could Vincenzo not see what these men were made of? How could he not see that despite Silvio Brunetti's horrendous actions, these men shared the same code of honor he himself lived by?

"In the big scheme of things, BFI and the villa matter very little. Both Massimo and I have learned that lesson the hard way. Neha and the babies, Natalie…the people who matter the most to us, we will still have them even if Vincenzo takes everything else, *si*?

"So you do what feels right to you. You do whatever your heart wants, Alex, and we're right behind you," Leo finished, reaching for her.

Alex went into his arms and buried her face in the familiar scent of him. This was what family meant. And this was what Vincenzo had never known. This was what she wanted to build with him, for her and for Charlie. And for V.

She was going to take the leap.

CHAPTER EIGHT

VINCENZO OPENED THE door and walked in. For a few seconds, he stood still, disoriented. He had given Alessandra more than a few days to recover. And she had taken to hiding in here, not just from him, but from everyone.

The conservatory was all glass on one side, giving a spectacular view of the lake. It was ablaze with lights and looked like a thunderstorm had raged through it and left utter chaos in its wake.

Boxes and boxes—some closed, the majority open with overflowing fabrics in every imaginable color—lay haphazardly around the vast room.

The surface of a dark mahogany table peeked from under a surfeit of sketchbooks and papers. Vincenzo picked up a book and rifled through hundreds of pages of sketches and designs, from elaborate evening dresses to stylish work shirts and suits. Two state-of-the-art sewing machines sat at a far corner and two mobile racks held dresses and other accessories in varying stages of completion.

A sheaf of papers had different versions of the same logo—a curlicued *A* and *A* wrapped around each other in different sizes. He was about to call out Alex's name when he heard a hiccup from the other end of the vast room.

Slowly, he made his way through the jumbled mess on the floor to the other end of the room, where a partition separated the work area from this second area. Sitting on the floor, with a half-empty wineglass and a bottle of red, was Alessandra. With her back to him.

Vincenzo took a few seconds to breathe through the desire that hit him like a gut punch.

She was wearing a white, wispy lace thing that plunged into a deep V at her back, showing off the toned musculature. Silky smooth, golden skin beckoned him for a touch.

While he watched in bemused fascination, she emptied her wineglass and hiccuped again.

"Alessandra?" He called out softly so as to not spook her.

She turned and threw him a glance over her shoulder, then looked away. In the brilliance of the lights, the tears in her eyes looked like crystals.

The slippery whisper of the silk of her dress made him look down. To sit comfortably, she had pulled fistfuls of fabric away from her long legs. The result was that it was gathered around her upper thighs all but baring every inch of her gorgeous body to his hungry gaze.

Vincenzo went to his knees next to her and gently placed his hand over her bare shoulder. Her skin felt freezing to his touch, though the room was comfortably warm. "Cristo, you're like ice!" He spread his fingers around desperate to warm her up.

"What?" She jerked, as if coming out of a trance. Dislodging his fingers in the process. "Oh, the cold, you mean? Yeah, I'm always cold," she said in a nasal voice that confirmed that she'd been crying.

For a few seconds, he got distracted by a memory from Bali. He had been startled awake from a deep sleep early one morning to find her wound around him. But what had woken him had been her cold feet tucked into the groove between his own ankles.

He had gone back to sleep, a smile on his lips, his heart brimming with a feeling he couldn't define. It had been a perfect morning.

"You know, when we met…it's so silly," she muttered and then laughed at herself. "I used to think it was so utterly romantic that you were always warm. As if there was a…volcano inside you. I actually took that as some sort of sign. That you'd always warm me up. For the rest of our lives.

"Can you believe the depth of my foolishness?"

He slid to the floor with not quite the economy he usually had, her words hitting him hard. The ache in them cutting deep. "It's not foolish, *cara mia.*"

She tucked an unruly lock of hair behind her ear, and he noticed the dangly diamond earrings glittering at her ears, the drop at the bottom kissing her shoulder every time she moved. An elegant choker—a matching set with the earrings, glimmered at her neck. Her dress, now that he was noticing things other than her painfully lovely face, was of a rich lace and ivory silk material. And it fit her to perfection.

In the beautiful white dress and the expensive jewelry, she looked like a bride.

She hadn't dressed up like this for their impromptu, impulsive wedding. He frowned. "Princess, is everything okay?"

"Hmm?"

He lifted the bottle to his gaze. Half-empty. "I didn't know you drank."

One bare shoulder rose and fell. "I don't usually, but I feel like I'm drowning. Tonight, I just want to not care."

He watched in increasing fascination as she took the wine bottle from him and swallowed a mouthful. A drop fell on the golden skin of her neck and rolled down into the valley of her breasts. He cursed under his breath, feeling the tightness in his trousers.

"You should be wary of me. I'm a mean drunk."

He smiled. "I'll take my chances, *bella*."

Trembling fingers dug through the rumpled mass of her hair. Her chest rose and fell. She rubbed her nose against her upper arm. The grief painted on her tight face sent alarm bells ringing inside his head. He took her hand in his, and pressed his thumb over her knuckles. In a rhythmic movement, back and forth.

"Talk to me, *cara mia*."

She shook her head.

"Afraid you'll spill your secrets?" he teased, faking a humor he didn't feel.

"I don't want to be responsible tonight."

"Then that is exactly why I should be here, *tesoro*. You can be as dangerous and impulsive as you want. Do your worst, Alex. I won't tell a soul."

The brown of her eyes seemed strangely feverish, and intent. Far too present to be truly drunk. The flimsy silk dress looked like it had been made for her. With her hair falling away from its knot and the dress a rumpled mess around her, she still managed to look delicately feminine. Fiercely sexy.

She licked her lower lip and held his gaze. "And if I want things I shouldn't want?"

His body hardened instantly. "Then we will indulge in that too."

When she leaned sideways suddenly, her breasts rubbed against his bicep. He felt electrocuted. Singed by the press of her soft flesh. Softly whispered words blew warm air over his neck. "And if the wine doesn't do its thing, will you help, V? Will you come inside me and—"

"Tell me about this room," he said loudly, cutting her off.

"Now who's running scared?" she taunted.

"I'll give you anything you want, Alessandra. Even if that is me pounding away inside you so that you can forget the grief I see in your eyes. I will let you use me any way you want, *bella*. But when that's done, when you wake up tomorrow with your body sore in the most delicious way, that grief will still be there. Waiting for you."

She wiped her mouth with the back of her hand. "I hate it when you get all sensible."

He let out a long groan. "I hate it when I have to be sensible when you're offering sex."

He saw her lips twitch at that. And it felt like a victory. A small one but one nonetheless. "This is my design studio. Leo had it built for me. He didn't want me to feel left out."

"Left out?" The mention of Leo's name cooled his ardor considerably.

"He had the old wine cellar transformed into a state-of-the-art tech lab for Massimo. Renovated the skeleton of an old greenhouse for himself. When he found out I was cramming yards of fabric in my bedroom, he had this conservatory remodeled into a design room for me." She ran a hand tenderly over the chaise longue, her voice catching. "I had only been here a year by then and I didn't trust him at all. When I asked him why, he simply said this was my home too and it should feel like that.

"He was maybe twenty. But then he's always been a protector at heart."

Vincenzo swallowed the bitter retort that sprang to his lips. "What do you design here?"

Her shoulders straightened with the deep breath she took, sending one silky strap falling off her shoulder. His fingers itched to trace the smooth expanse of that exposed skin, and follow it up with his mouth. "Evening dresses, mostly. I use vintage clothing and repurpose them to give them a new edge."

"Are you any good at it?"

"I'm brilliant at it," she answered, and he smiled. The few pieces he'd seen on the rack looked astoundingly beautiful even to his untrained eye. "But I... I have a love-hate relationship with it. For a long time, I pursued everything but design. Actually, I mostly hated it."

"Still do?"

A lone tear fell down her cheek. "No. Design is where my heart is. I just... I hated it because it was associated with her. Alyssa. It was the one thing she gave me."

"Your mother?"

"She was a very talented seamstress. An artist with a glorious vision, to be honest. Designing clothes was the one thing we had in common. She taught me when I was a little girl. All these boxes…they are hers. I wanted to donate the whole lot to charity and wash my hands of it. But… I couldn't help myself."

"She made this dress?" he asked, rubbing the silk between his fingers at the hem.

"I think so. It fits me almost perfectly. The lawyer overseeing their estate handed me the jewelry. I… Apparently, it was supposed to be her wedding gift to me."

"Alessandra—"

"But I didn't even tell her that I got married. I sent a postcard to Charlie from Bali, telling him, which she must have read. After I left you…she got in touch with me through Javier, wrote me a letter that he sent on. She wanted to meet you but I called her and told her we were too busy. I…told her she'd never been a part of my life and that it wasn't suddenly going to change. I was absolutely cruel. And a week later, she was gone. Poof. Just like that."

He took her hand in his and was again struck by how cold she was. Pulling it to his mouth, he blew warmth into it. "You had no way of knowing she'd be in an accident, Princess. Life is..."

"Unfair sometimes, yeah. She cheated on my stepfather. Did you know that? With my real father. Greta's second husband. She took off on holiday after they'd had a fight, met Carlos in Milan, had an affair and then returned to her husband, pregnant with me.

"And somehow, Steve forgave her. Except for the fact that there I was, the symbol of everything she'd done wrong, growing up in front of his eyes. Forever reminding him of his wife's infidelity."

"Was he cruel to you?"

"No." More tears drawing tracks on her cheeks. "Oh no, Steve was an honorable man, in his own way. It was her, you see. My mother never forgave herself for her mistake. I was the punishment for her sin."

He pressed his mouth to the back of her hand, feeling helpless against her pain. "You were only a child."

"There was always a coldness to her when I was growing up. A distance I could never cross. And finally, when I was thirteen, it all came out. The truth about my parentage. And I realized why she could never love me. So I reached out to Carlos and moved to Italy to live with him.

"I refused to live in a situation where I was

considered a weakness. A shameful secret. A weapon to be used in any argument."

"I'm sorry, Alex," Vincenzo whispered, the full scope of what he had done only just dawning on him now.

"I will not be a weapon to be used against them," she'd said again and again. *"I'm not a prize."*

"Do you know what's weird? I did so many things in life to enrage her. It wasn't enough to leave her.

"I became closer and closer to Greta. I took up modeling because I knew my mother would not approve. I…refused to even visit her, despite numerous calls from Steve. I thought I was hurting her. But really I only hurt myself."

"You did whatever you had to in order to survive."

She scrubbed at her tears roughly. "She reached out to me again after Charlie was born. I went, not to take her up on the olive branch, but because I was curious about Charlie. I was curious about how she would love this baby, if she did at all.

"And she did. I could see it in her eyes—he was a piece of her heart. She loved him like she never did me. And it broke my heart all over again.

"I love him so much now, but when he was first born I was so jealous of this small baby, Vincenzo. Can you believe it? This tiny human being had what she'd always denied me. Now she's gone. And Charlie's lost everything too."

"Shh…*tesoro*. Shh…none of this is your fault. Grief and guilt are a poisonous cocktail, *cara*," Vincenzo crooned as she broke into heart-wrenching sobs. He pressed his mouth to her temple and held her in a firm grip, his chest tight with an ache he couldn't name.

Her pain felt like his own, and his guilt that he'd only made it worse… It raked claws through him.

"How horrible does it make me that I don't truly miss her? I only miss what could have been…if we'd patched up our relationship."

He understood her so perfectly at that moment. The tangle of emotions that could choke your breath, a beautiful future slipping through your fingers and the helplessness it brought… His arms tightened around her and he rocked them both gently.

His mind turned to the implicit trust he had seen between Leo and Massimo Brunetti. The ethics they'd strived hard to instill in themselves were becoming clearer as he delved into BFI's operations ever since Silvio had been kicked out—with Greta's help, indeed—and Leo had taken over as CEO.

The bond the brothers shared despite Silvio Brunetti's cruelty toward his own sons… He'd seen the evidence of it with his own eyes.

Slowly, she turned into a languorous weight on his muscles. Sinking his fingers into her thick hair, he whispered sweet nothings in Italian. "You're human, *bella*. Not horrible. *What might have been* taunts us all."

Her fingers dug into his muscles, her mouth open against his shoulder. "You were right, you know."

"About what?" he whispered.

"I'm impulsive. I'm… I run away from hard situations. I take things on for all the wrong reasons. Sometimes, I'm…"

"What, Alessandra?"

"I'm scared, V. So much."

"About what, *bella*?"

She took a bracing breath. "What if I'm not the right person to raise Charlie, V? What if that jealousy I initially bore for him translates into my future actions? What if he can see it in me? What if he ends up believing I don't really love him? What if you were right, and I haven't thought this through completely?

"He's so scared right now. Only seven years old and he's been through so much already. I can't be another person who lets him down."

The fear in her voice cut Vincenzo deeply. With rough movements, he turned her until she was looking into his eyes. With her own puffy from her tears, her hair a ragged mess, she was still the most real thing he'd ever laid eyes on.

"Listen to me, Princess! You came storming back into this marriage just for him. Your love for him shines through in every word, every action. Trust me—he knows it.

"You don't know how amazing it is to see your strength, *cara*. You hated asking me for help, yet you did. Fighting me with everything you had. For Charlie. He's incredibly fortunate to have you."

He pressed another kiss into her hair, loving the silky tumble of it. Breathing in the essence of this woman who fought to do the right thing even when she was terrified. "It made me see things in you I've never seen before."

She stilled in his arms, her mouth a warm heat against the hollow of his throat. Her fingers dug into his muscles, but he welcomed the contact. "Like what?"

He shrugged, loath to share his doubts. Doubts she'd created in him.

"I thought of what a ferocious mother you'd be to any children we have," he finally answered.

She moved out of his arms and the loss of her warmth, her softness was acute.

He swallowed the urge to pull her back into his embrace. "You're one of those women around whom families are built. Your loyalty…staggers me. You give back everything you receive a hundredfold."

"And yet you would change the very core of me."

"No," he said with careful emphasis. "I only re-minded you that I had a right to your loyalty too."

She looked away and then back, and he noted the resolve in her eyes. He could practically see her emerge from this bout of intense grief, bent but not broken. Ready to take on whatever came next. And that determination aroused him as much as the beautiful dress offering him flashes of long, honey-colored limbs.

"Do you think we made a mistake?"

He didn't need to ask her to clarify. *"No."*

"I don't want to think of...us having children for a long time. Not until things are...settled. With Charlie. With us."

"That's fair," he said softly, swallowing away the instinctive protest.

"Would you forgive me if I did something like that?"

"Like what?"

"If I cheated on you, like my mother did to Steve. If I slept with another—"

"No!" His answer bounced off the walls and the floor, increasing in volume until it was re-verberating all around them.

The idea of losing Alessandra—to anything, much less another man... He felt shaken up from the inside. On levels he didn't understand. A few months ago, he'd been unaware of her existence and today—he had no words for all the feelings she evoked in him. Only that she was coming to mean so much more than he could ever have imagined.

Too much.

He took a deep breath. "What is it that you're trying to achieve with these ridiculous questions, *bella*?"

Defiance glared at him from those golden-brown depths. "Establishing boundaries, I suppose."

"That question is moot, Alessandra, because I don't believe you would ever do such a thing to me.

"Strip me bare of every rule I've ever lived by, *si*.

"Drive me crazy with your stunts to protect those two bastards from me, *si*.

"Make me pant after you like a damn dog in heat, *si*," he bit out, with a self-deprecating shake of his head. "But to cheat on me is to cheat on the life we want to build with each other—so, no, *bella*, that's not you."

And in that moment of vulnerability, of giving voice to things he'd never admitted before, even to himself, Vincenzo knew exactly how much she was changing him. Antonio had been right to worry.

From the first day he had met her, she had bowled him over with her beauty, but even more with her generosity, her integrity, her constant attempts to open herself up to others.

Alessandra made him want to be a different man. A better man.

A man who could open himself to the possibility of a relationship with his brothers, a man who gave others the second chance that he'd never been given. A man who could even consider forgiving the woman who had directly ruined his life, who had so thoroughly broken his mother's heart that she'd never recovered from it.

But he couldn't. He didn't know how. His path had been set so long ago that he didn't know how to choose a new one now. He didn't know how to be a man whose every waking thought was not filled with taking everything that had been denied him. How to be the man who had to face all the things he'd already done in the name of revenge.

"I was insanely jealous of Anna. How much she's a part of your past, a part of your present."

He wasn't shocked by the sudden turns their conversation took anymore. Neither did he derive any kind of satisfaction from the revelation. It had been a power trip to learn how much he affected Alex. But that was before. Before he realized that it worked both ways. Before he'd begun to view himself through her eyes. "She's firmly in my past. You're my future."

"I want to trust this so much. And not just for Charlie's sake. I need to believe in this marriage, V, in you.

"I want to stop caring about everything else. About Leo and Massimo, about BFI, about the entire world. I want what you promised me on the island, our life together."

His chest felt like it would burst open, so much emotion filled him. "All you need is to take a step toward me, *bella*, that final step."

"Then why does it feel like defeat?"

He shook his head. "I want your surrender, *bella*. Not your defeat."

Some unnamed emotion glittered in her eyes. Pulling the damned dress away from those legendary legs, she crawled toward him on her knees, flashes of bare golden flesh toying with him.

Her hands on his knees pushed them apart and she moved close, intoxicatingly close. The tips of her breasts brushed against his chest, her flat belly against his. Her fingers directed his hands to her thighs with no hesitation. The silk of her skin under his calloused fingers, the incredible scent of her teasing his nostrils... She was a feast he'd been denied for far too long.

"Alex, *bella*, we don't have to do this tonight, when you're still grieving—"

"No, I need this tonight. I need this now." Her hand moved to his neck, then upward to sink her fingers into his hair. Her warm lips skated over every inch of his face, branding him, staking a claim. "I don't want to think. I just want to feel."

Her breath was a warm benediction against his other cheek. He felt engulfed by her. Every moment, every day, she was beginning to own another piece of him. His breath began to come in harsh pants, as if he was trying to catch up to her. And he had a strangely feverish feeling that he would forever be trying to catch up.

"But sometimes I wonder if you're the devil or an angel," she whispered, the words flickering over his skin as she shifted that gloriously lithe body closer. And closer. Her lips descended toward his, her grip on his hair getting tighter. Until his head was tilted up to look into her eyes.

"All I care is that you're mine." That first press of her mouth against his, after so long, sizzled right through his skin. "Please, V…say you're mine."

Words came and fell away from his mouth as she looked deep into his eyes. He considered and threw away platitudes that had no meaning, lies that would damage the surrender she was giving him. Surrender he wasn't sure he deserved.

And then they came, so easily, slumbering awake from some deep place he didn't even know existed within himself. They burned in his chest, lit a fiery path through his throat as he tried to process the weight of the feeling. Of how unprepared he was for them.

"I'm yours, *bella*. Like I've never been anyone else's."

She came at him like a wild storm then, pushing into him, pressing into him, shaking the very ground he stood on. Her mouth… *Madre di Dio*, in all the wildness, her mouth was a lush escape. A warm invitation to heaven.

"And I'm yours. All of me is yours," she whispered frantically against his mouth, a benediction he hadn't even known he'd been waiting for.

Vincenzo cupped her hips, eager for more of her taste. He growled when she sank her teeth into his lower lip and then swiped that wicked tongue over it. Desire pounded at him, urging him to pull the flimsy dress up and away, until he could reach the hot apex of her sex. Patience was a hard-earned battle as he buried his mouth in her neck. The warm, sweet taste of her skin calmed him even as it aroused him, and he nipped at it with his teeth.

She rocked her hips into him at that, making him uncomfortably hard in his trousers. "I missed you, *bella*. I missed this with you," he whispered, licking the tiny mark on her neck. "But I'll be damned if I do this here, on the floor like an eager schoolboy when I can think of a hundred different ways of torturing you for all the months I've waited."

Her laughter enveloped him. She clung to him as he easily pushed them both off the floor. He was stunned at how much he had missed that laughter of hers too. The open joy she found in the most intimately carnal things he did to her.

"I would have much preferred the floor if for nothing else that it clearly says you can't wait until we get to the bedroom to have me."

"Ah...but I want to take my time with you. You cut our honeymoon disastrously short and there's so many things we still have to discover about each other, *si*?"

She shivered at that and he took her mouth roughly, thrusting his tongue into the warm cavern of her mouth. His muscles burned with the need for more... More contact, more friction, more of her. She and him... It had never been just sex between them.

Antonio had seen it. Had warned him.

And yet, Vincenzo couldn't even imagine controlling this somehow, much less walking away from it.

CHAPTER NINE

"I'M YOURS, BELLA."

Alessandra hugged those words close as Vincenzo deposited her on her bed and devoured her with those penetrating eyes. The luxurious sheets were cold against her skin, a startling contrast to the heat pouring off the man, looking down at her as if she were his downfall and salvation all at the same time. For long, painfully pregnant moments, he did nothing but look at her. Pushing up on her elbows, Alex returned his stare without hesitation.

Like I have been never been anyone else's. Those quiet words resonated around them, explosive in the silence, though she knew they had been given reluctantly.

Her breath hitched in her throat as urgent hands landed on her knees and pushed them indecently apart, making space for himself between her legs. The silk of her dress whispered sinuously against the sheets as those very same hands found her buttocks and pulled her to the edge of the bed. Until his hips kissed her inner thighs. His fingers dug into her bottom as he tilted her up. Until his erection glided against the hottest part of her.

Alex thrust involuntarily, the shape and weight of that hardness making her feverishly delirious for more. Fingers clutching the sheets, she let out a moan when Vincenzo rocked against her, his hips doing that wickedly erotic thing that had made her go crazy that first time.

Hungry gaze holding hers captive, he pushed aside her flimsy thong and traced a finger up and down her wet folds. Circled the hot place she needed him to touch without quite giving in to her.

"Please, V," she whispered, desperate for the clawing under her skin to subside.

"You mean this is better than your new technological friend?" It sounded like a tease, but the fire in his eyes told her it was anything but. His hands cupped her knees. Bent over her like that, he looked like a warrior intent on plunder.

Alex could barely hold the whimper at the loss of the acute pressure. "You never let me finish the story that night," she murmured now.

"Si?" His tongue licked at her mouth, his flat, hard abdominal muscles gliding temptingly against her wet folds. She slid up and down on the bed, and he rewarded her with a movement of his own.

Alex groaned, her lower belly corkscrewing at the contact.

"Finish it now, Alessandra."

The quiet command sank into her pores. Alex opened her eyes and smiled. "I had an orgasm that night, yes. But it felt empty without your whispered commands in my ear, without your body pushing down on me, without the warmth of your skin against mine... Nothing feels as good as you do, V. Nothing in the entire wide world."

His answering grin, full of wicked charm and self-satisfied arrogance, was so devastatingly gorgeous that she reveled in it.

And then his hand drifted down again, down her belly to that aching place, rubbing the sensitive bundle of nerves with those wickedly clever fingers. His thumb drew erotic circles while he thrust a finger inside her.

"*Cristo*, I've missed this warmth of yours," he said, his gaze devouring every dazed expression in her eyes. "Make those sounds for me, *bella*."

His fingers moved again with a mesmerizing rhythm that lit up every nerve center in Alex's body. When he bent down and took her mouth in a sensual tangle of a kiss, she clung to him, her body writhing under him, chasing that rhythm.

"Tell me what you need," he asked, like he'd done every time they made love. Every time, he learned her body by making her learn her own.

Every time, he pushed her to new discoveries about herself and what she liked. "Tell me what will make this all the sweeter for you, *tesoro*."

"Touch me here," she said, cupping her aching breasts. Just imagining his mouth there had sent her off the edge that night she'd had her empty orgasm.

"Pull the straps down."

Alex raised her hands automatically, every cell in her body attuned to his demands, ready to surrender to his every wish. Slowly, with movements that made those gray eyes darken into something indecently erotic, she hitched each index finger under the straps and flicked them off her shoulders. But the straps didn't fall all the way down and she locked them about her elbows by stretching her hands toward him.

"I want to touch you first," she demanded in a husky voice, knowing that once he got his hands on her flesh, her all too willing flesh, she was going to be cast into a vortex of sensations. Of need and pleasure.

If she wanted to take a little of him, wanted to ensure he was as far gone as she in this, she needed to do it now. She needed to touch, caress, kiss, every inch of him before he took over.

"You haven't tormented me enough, *bella*?" he said, his thumb tracing her collarbone, while the other dipped into her wetness, and out, in a mesmerizing rhythm that threatened to steal her resolve.

Fingers on his wrist, she stilled his hand. "I want to be more than a participant in this. I want to take something from you too."

He dipped his head in a sudden movement and took her mouth in a rough kiss that mocked his control. "You think I haven't given myself to this...to you?" he whispered against her mouth, his breath melded with her own.

"But whatever you give," she said, pressing her face into his throat, tasting his skin, "it's not..."

He didn't let her finish. As if he knew she was about to say. That whatever he gave, it wasn't enough until she had his heart.

She couldn't bear to look at him, to see the answer in his eyes.

And he... For the first time since she'd known him, Vincenzo didn't meet her gaze. He capitulated. Lost the battle, she knew, instead of the war.

Long lashes hiding the expression in his eyes, he brought her hands to his shirt. "Then do what you will with me, *Princess*."

Alex blinked away at the hotness that threatened behind her eyes. She was going to live for what she did have.

Him.

This.

She was going to build the family she'd never had. She was going to give it her all, regardless.

She didn't hesitate as she unbuttoned his shirt and pulled it out of his trousers. Almost frantic with the need to touch, she pushed the shirt off his shoulders and ran her hands, palms down, from the tight muscles in his shoulder to his jutting collarbone and then down, tracing the ridges of his chest to the rock-hard muscles of his abdomen.

Up and down, left and right, she zigzagged her hands, her cold hands, over his warm, taut skin. Though he stayed still, she didn't miss the way his breathing became shallow, even harsh, with each path she traced on his skin. Pushing herself up, up, she followed the path her hands traced on his chest and abdomen with her mouth.

He tasted of sweat and salt and something so gloriously masculine that she whimpered. This close to him, each breath he inhaled and exhaled hit the upper curves of her breasts in a tantalizing rhythm that had her nipples tauten, begging for more.

She tested the give of his muscle with her teeth, and an animalistic grunt escaped his mouth when she gently bit his pectorals. She busied her hands with, first his belt, and then the clasp of his trousers. And still she was aware that he was letting her. His control, she had no doubt, was on a short leash tonight. Almost at the end. But then, she had given him her surrender, unconditional surrender, and she had known from the first moment she'd met him, that Vincenzo would gift her with the entire universe in return for that surrender. She shivered now, even as his warm skin somehow diffused its heat into her skin.

All thoughts fled her brain when she pushed his trousers off his hips and instinctively reached for the hardness that she wanted. Again, that guttural grunt, that sharp hiss of an inhale, when she touched the thick length of him.

Steel coated in velvet, he lengthened and hardened further even as she wrapped her fingers around him. As a man, he was just the same, she realized. Smooth words, gorgeous smile, and at the core of him, he was unshakable in his resolve, in his quest toward revenge.

If destruction was what he wanted, then she would give it to him.

She turned her fingers into a fist and moved it up and down that hard length, as she'd done in those first few days when they'd been busy discovering each other's bodies like explorers on some new land. But there had been no challenge between them then.

Only an intrinsic need for each to discover what gave the other the most pleasure. She rubbed the soft head with her thumb in movements that mimicked the gentle torture he'd rained over her.

Head thrown back, eyes closed, that lean, hard chest breathing deep, he groaned out loud.

But she wanted even more. She was determined to wrest the last of his control from him. Until he too stood in the wake of this thing between them, stripped and vulnerable.

"Tell me your deepest fantasy," she coaxed, the very thought of that steely length inside her making her sex ache with want.

"This," he said, his face bathed in moonlight from the French windows. He clasped her jaw, his thumb tracing her lower lip. His other hand tightened in her hair, tugging, raising her face up. "You...like this. All mine."

"Me...doing what?" she demanded, scooting to the edge of the bed. She pulled her legs up and under her, and propped herself up on her elbows, bringing her face to the height of that hard evidence of his arousal. Leaning down, she blew on it.

He tensed. "Do it," he whispered after what felt like an eternity.

"Do what?" she threw back, fluttering her eyelashes at him. "Ask me nicely."

"Take me in your mouth now," he commanded, but there was a desperation to it.

Falling onto her knees, she obeyed.

Another loud groan ripped through the air around them. Digging her nails into his hard thighs for purchase, Alex licked the entire length of him, up and down. A filthy curse came next, filling her with power and arousal, a cocktail that vibrated through her.

Then she took him in her mouth and his fingers plunged into her hair, giving her instructions in a hoarse voice that rumbled right through her.

She had no idea how long he gave her free rein of his body, but she loved having him like this. Had no sense of time or the world around them as she played with the evidence of what she did to him. For a few minutes, or it could have been hours, he was putty in her hands.

Every thrust and jerk of his hips as she licked the length of him with her hands at the base, every curse gritted out through a tense jaw, every tug of his fingers in her hair urging her to go faster and harder, was music to Alex's ears.

"Enough, *bella*!" he declared, and within moments, Alex was lying back on the bed, her dress rucked up to her hips, and Vincenzo eyeing her as if he meant to consume her.

With her golden-brown hair spread out on pristine white sheets, her eyes glittering in her flushed face, Alessandra was the most beautiful thing Vincenzo had ever seen.

Her bare breasts with those plump brown nipples, the taut flat belly with the white bridal dress rucked up to her waist, and the long, toned legs, the strip of hair covering the wet warmth he desperately wanted to bury himself in... And that mouth, that gloriously pink, pouty mouth that had licked and stroked him right to the edge of heaven...

If she'd asked him for something tonight, he wouldn't deny her. Yet even that warning thought couldn't clear the fog of desire claiming his senses.

But nothing could compare to the expression in her eyes as she looked at him now. As if he were her safe harbor in the midst of a storm. As if he were the only thing that could save her. As if he were as necessary to her as air.

He stepped out of his trousers and filled his hands with her butt cheeks and pulled her close. A light coating of sweat shone on her body. He ran his hands from the sleekly soft skin of her inner thighs to the toned muscle of her midriff, up, up, to the perfect globes of her breasts. Followed that with his mouth, licking and nipping as he went.

Every time, he pulled the skin between his teeth, she jerked and thrust up with her hips. And he got a little harder. When he finally reached her mouth, he thrust his tongue into hers and she clung to him, panting, sobbing.

And then he began the journey back down, drinking in the silky softness of every inch of her. He pinched the plump nipples between his fingers and tugged, just as he knew she liked.

She bowed off the bed, her body arcing like

she'd been hit by lightning. He bent his head and flicked his tongue over one tight bud and teased her. Her hips, her breasts, everything jerked up toward him as if she wanted to burrow into his skin and remain there. He wanted to tell her that she was already there. That she had gotten under the skin of a man whom nothing had ever touched before.

That he didn't know how to dislodge her. That already he was seeing things differently, seeing a future for himself that jarred violently with his present path.

"Please… Vincenzo, please. I need your mouth there," she said, not in supplication though. But with demand, with fierce need. He had loved that about her. She demanded pleasure as fiercely as she gave it. She demanded it as if it were her due.

"With pleasure, *cara mia*," he said, and closed his lips over her sensitive nipples.

Tremors took over her entire body. Holding her lower body tight against his own, he alternated between both breasts, kissing and licking, sucking and blowing air on the wet tips, until they were swollen and glistening in the moonlight. Slowly, he brought her down to the bed and tilted her hips up toward him.

"Keep your eyes open, *bella*," he instructed, wanting her to see what she did to him.

He rubbed himself in her wetness, the erotic glide sending long moans out of their mouths. A shudder racked his entire body when he entered her in a deep thrust that took him home. Alessandra cried out and he stilled inside her, holding her to him.

"Damn it! Did I hurt you—"

"No." Her lithe body stretched under him, as if she wanted to feel him everywhere. "I just..." She locked those beautiful eyes on him, and Vincenzo knew this was the home he'd been chasing for most of his life. "I just forgot how...achy this feels. How thoroughly you fill me up. How well you know what I like."

And then she smiled and raised her hips in an experimental thrust and an arrow of pleasure shot up the base of his spine. But it wasn't just pleasure as he started moving in short, fast thrusts. He had no words for what it felt like when her gaze moved over him, her fingers tracing each feature.

It had felt like home that first time too. It had felt like nothing he'd ever known before. Excitement and arousal, pleasure and warmth, satisfaction and peace—all the things he'd never had in his life, he'd found in her embrace. Only he hadn't seen it then.

And now it was too late.

There was no sense of him when he was inside her—his goal, his ambition, his cause, his revenge— everything disappeared. When she clasped his face in her hands and kissed his mouth. When her hips thrust up in a desperate need to be closer to him. When she was pulling him irrevocably into the fabric of her own life. Her loved ones, her family, her goals, her generous heart.

She made him drown; she pulled the ground away from under him.

"More, please. Everything you have, V," she demanded, her core contracting and releasing him, her thighs slapping against his hips with every damp slide of his body against her.

Every tiny pulse of her body hit him as he pulled out and then thrust back in again. Every muscle in his body curled against the next, bracing for the surfeit of pleasure.

But he knew Alessandra's surrender did not come without a price.

Even if she didn't ask it, even if she didn't demand her due, Vincenzo knew there would soon be a day when he would not be able to pay it.

How had Alex forgotten how transformative sex was between Vincenzo and her? The magic that seemed to be created when they came together? The rightness of it?

It was what had driven her to marry a man who'd been a complete stranger.

Alex whimpered at the emptiness as he pulled out completely but was rewarded not a moment later, when he climbed up onto the bed, on all fours, a primal need etched onto his stunning features. A drop of sweat dripped from his forehead and plopped onto the swell of her breast and his hungry eyes followed it. As if she were prey, and he meant to consume her.

And then he was back on her again, over her, inside her, around her. His weight on top of hers both a safe haven and a vortex of thrill at the same time.

He yanked her closer and thrust inside her, a deep growl rumbling out of him. Alex cried out at the welcoming hardness, at the incredible friction. She was lifted off the bed, hands on her buttocks pulling her up until she was astride his lap. The bare economy with which he arranged her to his liking, the strength in his lean corded limbs only amplified the thrall he had her under.

Alex wrapped her arms around his damp back, feeling him everywhere inside her in this position. The rub of her breasts against his chest, the intimacy of locking gazes with him deepened her pleasure to an unbearable level.

He was so hard and pulsing inside her, his breath warming every inch of her neck, his scent—a sweaty, masculine combination that filled her very senses. Their mouths locked again in a devastatingly hungry communion that she knew now would never be enough. She held on to him as if she could hold his heart to hers this way. She wanted to stay like that forever, in his arms, surrounded by him, and let time stretch from this moment to the next and the next.

Alex buried her face in his shoulder. Damp, soft, warm, he was an explosive taste on her tongue.

"Look at me, *bella*."

She squeezed her eyes closed tighter, afraid of what he would see in them. Afraid of the wide chasm of need that opened up inside her when he held her like this, when he moved inside her.

"Please, V. Finish me off, won't you? I want to come so desperately I feel like I'll die if I don't," she said, imbuing every inch of want that thrummed through her into her words.

"I won't move inside you while you hide away from me, *bella*," he growled, a vein of tension in his voice. Every inch of him was taut under her fingers. He strummed a line of music on her bare back, his mouth at her temple. "I have become used to seeing myself in your eyes, Alessandra. I have become used to drowning in your gaze."

Her head jerked up at the pure need in those words.

So she let their mouths tangle, their tongues lap at each other, their teeth nip at each other until it was hard to tell where she ended and where he began. His heart was a violent drum against her breast, his body a damp, sleek fortress of demand as he thrust up.

With each grunt of his, Alex moved up and down while need corkscrewed in her belly.

She let the sounds and scents that their bodies created together lead her on and on until no rational thought was possible. Vincenzo murmured, "That's it, Alex. Stay with me."

And then he was pressing her back into the bed, and holding her down with the thrust of his hips. Alex gave herself over to it as he rode her body hard, chasing his pleasure.

Alex opened her mouth against his bicep and dug her teeth in, knowing what he liked. Wanting him lost to this madness like her. "Faster, please, V," she sobbed, her release an ephemeral breath away.

Her legs draped over his shoulders, his pelvis rubbed sinuously against her in exactly the right place every time he thrust.

"Touch yourself, *bella*. Come with me," he commanded, and Alex moved her hand down from his chest to the apex of her thighs.

Eyes wide-open, she held Vincenzo's gaze, and the emotion she saw there pushed her over the edge. "Oh," she whispered, on and on, again and again, into his damp skin as her release flung her open wide.

There was nothing like the magic of her climax when he was inside her, something he made them both work for every time. Nothing like being swept up by the storm of pleasure that drove him toward his own.

Her release continued in short pulses. Vincenzo deepened his thrusts—once, twice, thrice—and fell onto her with a fierce growl. Her name on his lips was a crooning whisper that settled like a blanket of contentment over her naked skin. Alex wrapped her arms around him and held on, as if the physical act somehow guaranteed more than that. As if…

No, she wasn't going there. This was all she needed. She'd chosen this path, she'd chosen him, and she'd stick to it come what may.

He stayed on top of her like that, for long, perfect moments. "You okay?" he asked finally.

Alex turned toward him and smiled. "More than okay," she whispered, and he took her mouth in a rough, snarly kiss that warmed her all the way to her cold toes.

CHAPTER TEN

VINCENZO CAME AWAKE with a start.

Falling asleep anytime before predawn was such an unusual thing for him that he felt disoriented for several minutes after opening his eyes.

Restful sleep had always been impossible for him. For the longest time, he had forced himself to stay awake to keep an eye on his mother, afraid that she might do some irreparable damage to herself if he fell asleep.

Once he had achieved a measure of financial freedom to hire a round-the-clock nurse to ensure his mother's care, it had been too late. His insomnia by then had been entrenched, a by-product of the numerous nights he'd spent through relentless years, building his fortune.

After that, he had a financial empire to rule.

But now, after only a few nights here in the villa, he was so used to the warm, languorous weight of Alessandra's limbs vined around him that sleep came easily. To go to bed without her now seemed like a dreary prospect, even temporarily.

The thought disquieted him enough to rouse him completely. With slow movements, he disengaged her long limbs from his.

He swept a lock of hair away from her face and ran his fingers lightly over those blade-like cheekbones, his heart a strangely weighty thing in his chest. She moaned and rolled and the duvet slipped, offering glimpses of a smooth silky shoulder and the upper curve of a breast.

Instantly, he felt the answering tightness of his own body. *Cristo*, it had been six days since he'd found her in that conservatory, and they'd spent most of those six days burning through the heat between them.

It showed no signs of abating. He had been insatiable, and she'd been there with him every step of the way. Wrenching himself away from the temptation she offered, he pulled on sweatpants and a T-shirt, made his way out of the bedroom.

The long corridors were quiet, the marble cold against his feet. He was not surprised when he arrived at the huge study, the seat of Leonardo's power, the seat from where centuries of the masters of this revered dynasty had used their power.

To this day, Vincenzo still hadn't figured out the older Brunetti, the true heir to all this. Massimo was more open, full of a caustic wit that

made even Vincenzo smile. But in Leonardo…
He could see shades of himself.

"Imagining yourself here?" came a voice behind him.

He turned to find Greta Brunetti standing just inside the door, her shoulders stiff.

"Imagination is for dreams out of your reach. This chair, this study, this house…it's all within my grasp already. If you must know," he said, surprised at his own rancor spewing into his words, but continuing anyway, "I was wondering what I would wreck first. This study, or the tall towers of BFI."

She paled, and he felt a glimmer of regret. Only a glimmer.

"What do you want, Mr. Cavalli?"

Her formal address raked at something inside him, but he refused to show it. "The time for action is long past for you," he said, leaning against the massive dark oak table and crossing his ankles.

Her claw-like hands folded tightly against her midriff. "It's never too late to realize one is wrong. Never too late to make amends."

Shock drenched him, stealing away his anger. "Ah…it's your fear of destruction speaking."

"No, it's not. Whatever you're planning, it has little effect on me at this stage in life. But Alessandra, if I could do anything to—"

"She's mine. I won't give her up for anything

in this world. She made her choice again not six days ago. She makes the choice to be mine every night," he threw at the old woman shamelessly.

"I know that. I've already lost her respect, and that's worse than anything you can do to me. But I ask you to remember that she's an innocent in all this."

"My mother was an innocent too."

"I did what I thought was right at that time for my family. For years, I put up with my son's antics. Tried to patch up his actions, dealt with the consequences. I had become hardened to everything else—I had no mercy or kindness or even love left in me, because he drained it all away.

"I only did my duty by Leo and Massimo. I… starved them of affection—"

"They had a roof over their heads, food in their bellies, shelter against storms. I had nothing," Vincenzo threw at her, his chest rising and falling.

Not even a childhood. That was the price he had paid for her mercilessness.

He had never been allowed to be a child.

Her chin jerked down, and the old woman looked away for long, painful minutes. He ran a shaking hand through his hair. "I will grant you that your grandsons are not the monsters I thought them."

Alessandra's faith in Leo and Massimo had

not been bought with all this wealth or by favors, Vincenzo was learning with each day.

It was a hard pill to swallow: the genuine affection she shared with both men, being here in the seat of the family's power for generations, being the outsider.

But worse was the realization—like a shard of glass stuck in his throat—that that affection, that bond with the Brunetti brothers, should have been his too. To see them over the breakfast table, to understand the easy camaraderie between them, to feel like the outsider when he had just as much right to that bond with them... It was a special kind of torment.

Alessandra's hope that somehow he could cross the divide between them and build that bond with them—now, after everything he'd done to bring them down, after all the bitter hatred he'd nursed for them for over two decades... It was just that—a naive, pathetic hope that he refused to indulge in.

"That was despite my presence in their life," Greta added softly, and Vincenzo turned to her with a frown. "You are under a grand delusion if you think Leo and Massimo had a nurtured upbringing in this home.

"After dealing with Silvio's cruel antics and the fallout for so many years, I had nothing left to give them. They grew up to be honorable men, despite their abusive father and me.

"It was only when I married Alessandra's father, Carlos, that I realized…how many mistakes I had made. How I had let my son and his actions change me into this…bitter woman who had not even a kind word for her grandsons."

Vincenzo refused to indulge the thin thread of sympathy that reverberated within him at the woman's words.

Nothing, nothing could forgive what she'd done to his mother and him. This was all Alessandra's doing. The blasted woman was changing how he saw things, was undoing him at a cellular level.

"*Per piacere*, Vincenzo, do not…hurt Alessandra."

"I'm to believe you care for her that much?"

"*Si*, I do. She gave me a chance to be someone else. To redeem myself. To…find love in my heart again. Please…"

"Promise me you won't use me in this battle of yours?" Alessandra had asked him just before they'd danced at Antonio's party.

And he'd given her his word. And yet, if he could end this war he'd waged all the sooner, all the more cleanly, by using her, if he could avoid the total destruction he'd originally planned, wouldn't she ultimately be grateful to him? Wouldn't she understand why he'd done it?

His thoughts ran away from him like a runaway freight train before he could hold on to one and process it.

If, once he'd pulled apart BFI, he left this house intact instead of bringing it down—this house that she loved so much, this house that had been her safe harbor... If Alessandra and he could build that family of theirs here, if they could have a fresh start in this place where once his dreams had been crushed... Wasn't his revenge still complete?

Wasn't justice served then?

"If she's that important to you, then prove it to me," he said, pushing away the quiet voice of conscience that threatened to take over if he let it.

Her skin whitened to such deathly paleness that Vincenzo felt a twinge of remorse. He had hated this woman so much for so long, and yet she looked like nothing but a husk of the person from his memory, who had with one merciless decision, ruined his childhood, his mother's sanity.

The years in between should have etched that hardness she had showed them that day onto her face and yet, her eyes shone with conviction. With love, he realized, a cold chill taking over his skin.

Love that Alessandra had created in this old woman's bitter heart.

Love and something like the longing that he

had glimpsed in Alessandra's eyes when she looked at him.

It was the most terrifying thing he'd ever seen. Because he was beginning to realize he didn't deserve it. It amplified into an urgent drumbeat in his blood—this need to finish what he'd started soon. Before it was too late.

"How?" the old woman asked, pulling him out of his own murky thoughts.

"Ask your grandson to step down as CEO of BFI."

"Leonardo has worked far too hard for far too many years to just give up now."

"Then *make him*."

"It's not—"

"Throw your support behind me at the next board meeting."

The old woman swayed on her feet and reached for the support of the table. "If I back you, Leonardo will lose the controlling majority."

"It is a far better fate than what I had initially decided for them both."

Her eyes held his in a defiant challenge, an almost mirror image of the resolve he spied in his own eyes. A resemblance that he wanted to deny at any cost, and yet it was there. "For two centuries, only a Brunetti sat on that chair." A hint of that Brunetti arrogance crept back into the woman's words, her spine straightening. "It's against tradition—"

"The choices you have are very simple," Vincenzo said with a shrug. Any doubts he might have indulged in washed away at the flash of that Brunetti arrogance in her eyes. "Either keep BFI intact by throwing your support behind me or see all of it torn into pieces like I initially planned.

"With the first choice, you might even save Alessandra some heartache in the process. That's what you came to ask me for, remember? That I don't hurt Alessandra in all this."

"And you would use my affection for her this way?"

"Your words, your actions created the man I am today. You only have yourself to blame."

"This will break her heart. You're truly—"

"My father's son, *si*? So I have been told. You'd better not tell her then." He refused to think of what would happen if Alessandra found out. He refused to let it sway him when he was so close to being done. *Cristo*, he so badly wanted to be done. He wanted that future life with Alessandra to begin right now. "Alessandra has already chosen me. Chosen a future with me," he said, letting the old woman see his victory. "If I take over BFI, this can all be over for her too. She won't feel so caught up between her past and her future."

He left the room without looking back, a sort of desperation filling him to see Alessandra in that bed. To hold her. To reassure himself that she...

He felt dirty. As if he completely deserved the loathing he'd seen in the old woman's eyes.

He reached the bedroom, and only then did air fill his lungs. He stripped fast and got back into the bed. Like clockwork, Alessandra reached for him and burrowed into him. Only then did his heart slow its savage race.

"Did we make a mistake, V?"

Had she asked him that only a few nights ago?

And he realized with a sinking dread that the answer was yes. He had made a mistake. He had involved a woman who deserved far better than him in his life. He had tangled with a woman who deserved to be loved, to be worshipped. Who didn't deserve to be used as currency against the woman she loved.

But as Alex wrapped her long limbs around him, as she pulled him over her sweet temptation of a body, as she took his mouth in a warm kiss, as he lazily thrust into her and built them both up into that delicious frenzy again, Vincenzo didn't even consider for one second if he could give her up to fix the mistake. Release her from his life.

He couldn't. He wouldn't.

Because she was his. Not the prize he'd once so foolishly thought her. But so much more.

His salvation and his sanctuary.

Alessandra was still riding the high of the evening as she walked into the New York penthouse, put away her portfolio, stripped and went into the shower in quick succession. Her skin tingled as she thought of seeing Vincenzo again after four long days apart, of returning the favor he had done her in the one way she knew he would appreciate.

The warm spray from the powerful jet invigorated her as she smiled, anticipation building like a current inside her.

Thank God he'd had Anna tell her, even if it had been a bit dicey, at the last moment to bring her design portfolio with her. That the surprise he'd arranged for her was a dinner meeting with the talented CEO of an up-and-coming couture house with its base in New York City—a meeting Alessandra had been pursuing for more than a month now with no success.

One of the numerous things that Vincenzo arranged in her life, with an incredible arrogance that sometimes stole her breath.

But for all the initial protest that rose up inside her at his high-handedness, Alessandra could never fail to see the intentions—usually good intentions, behind his presumptuous actions. Like this meeting with the trendsetting CEO.

She had only just admitted to herself, and whispered to him that night in her design studio a few weeks ago, that she wanted to launch herself as a designer. That she wanted to launch her own label as Alessandra & Alyssa—a label that would commemorate her mother's artistic vision and the peace that Alex had finally found after all these years.

It had been a painful internal journey but she knew it was the right thing to do—to acknowledge that her mother had loved her, in her own way, to use the talent and vision for design she'd inherited from Alyssa to build her own company.

Neither could she lie to herself anymore. Vincenzo had helped her achieve that peace. For a man who was so ruthless about so many things, he had been insightful and kind when it was her grief they were dealing with.

As soon as he'd understood what she'd wanted, he had set in motion so many meetings for her all across the globe. Using his connections.

Not that Alessandra lacked a network. But his was just bigger and better, she reluctantly admitted to herself.

For example this particular CEO—his couture house had been in the news of late for its ethical practices, for designing couture using recycled vintage wear, and for its fair trading policies with so many third world countries where it sourced the vintage fabrics. It would be the dream of a couture house to launch her first line with. But even with her connections and her agent's clout, Alessandra hadn't been able to acquire a meeting with the man.

No sooner had she revealed her frustration to

Vincenzo, there it was in her calendar, a meeting with that CEO.

And it had gone tremendously well, she and the man instantly hitting it off.

At least the nausea that had threatened her all day—she frowned...no, all week, actually—hadn't ruined the evening. Victor Emmanuel had been both excited and amazed by her portfolio, and Alessandra couldn't wait to begin working with such a brilliant visionary. Couldn't wait to see her label launched—a future woven from the threads of the past.

When she had laughingly mentioned Vincenzo twisting his arm to get her the appointment, he had, with a sudden seriousness, admitted that he was the one who owed Vincenzo a favor. Because her husband had been the very man who had helped him raise seed capital in what was a cutthroat industry all those years ago.

Every time Alex thought she knew Vincenzo, that she understood him, he threw a monkey wrench into it.

She toweled her damp hair and pulled a robe on, a strange lethargy gripping her. Barefoot, she walked into the bedroom of the penthouse that challenged the New York City skyline with its magnificence.

They had been here for three weeks now, and Alessandra had discovered she didn't want to return home. God, she wanted to stay here forever, away from Italy and the myriad demands it placed on her husband's time, energy and even loyalty.

It had been a glorious few weeks' respite, and she was loath to see it come to an end.

Since she had made her choice, since she had decided that she couldn't let his war with Leonardo and Massimo break her apart into so many pieces, just as she'd guessed, Vincenzo, in return for that surrender, had been busy placing the world at her feet in return.

And it hadn't been just his support, his encouragement, and the use of his extensive network when it came to launching her new career. He had barely returned from a weeklong conference in Beijing when she had been ready to leave for New York to see Charlie again.

A few hours with him at the most had been what she'd been hoping for. Because, once she had stopped lying to herself, once she'd stopped fighting herself, she had admitted how much she missed him.

How much she missed their talks about their careers, about their futures, their long, lazy nights, where she kept thinking that one more night, one more time would calm the fire that raged between them. But it did not. It was as if a different Vincenzo—charming, contented, that Vincenzo she had first met in Bali—had emerged again since she had thrown her lot in with him.

The only blip, the only thing that marred her near-perfect happiness was his past. He refused to even talk about his mother or his ongoing battle to gain the controlling stock of BFI. As long as Alessandra didn't broach either of those subjects—and she made a conscious effort not to—he was everything she could have ever asked for.

No, he was more than she'd ever expected to have in her life.

A week ago, he had surprised her by joining her on the flight to New York, even though she knew he'd been busy with his own global interests.

He'd been incredibly patient when Charlie had refused to even meet his gaze, reassuring Alex that he knew how to handle the little boy.

He had also made time to spend an entire day with Charlie and her, arranging an impromptu picnic at Central Park, playing the tourist with them. At the end of the day, Charlie had asked Vincenzo when he'd visit again.

"What's important to you is important to me," he'd said simply when she had inquired.

Except the Brunettis.

Even a single mention of either Greta, or Leo or Massimo, and instantly, he transformed into a man Alex didn't understand. A man that she was increasingly afraid for. How long could a person sustain such hatred, such anger and not be changed by it? When it was finally over, what would be left for her?

Alex sighed and poured out a glass of water when the private elevator pinged behind her. Like a teenage girl, her heart beat faster, her skin prickled with anticipation as footsteps echoed down the sitting room and then into the bedroom where she stood by the French doors.

She hadn't seen him in four days. A meager four days, and yet it felt like a lifetime. "Hey," she said, leaning her wobbling knees against the cold glass, her throat already parched again.

He stood still, framed by the rounded archway and suddenly the distance between them felt like a chasm. A chasm he was creating between them.

"What's wrong?" she asked, knowing that she was overreacting and yet unable to stop the thread of fear unspooling in her belly.

"You said you wouldn't interfere in this anymore. You said you'd chosen your path, that you chose me."

"I did."

"Then what do you call all the maneuverings you've set into motion behind my back? I can't leave you alone for a few days? *Cristo*, no wonder Antonio thinks I'm whipped."

"What maneuverings? What are you talking about?" She had never seen him so angry and his anger brought out hers. Suddenly, the magic she'd found in the city with him seemed to evaporate right in front of her eyes. "Also, I'd appreciate it if you didn't discuss our marriage with that bitter old man."

His eyes narrowed. "That bitter old man is the only father figure I've ever had. That bitter old man is the only reason I stand before you as a successful businessman instead of a criminal languishing behind bars."

As quickly as it came, her anger got swept away. She reached him and clasped his jaw in her hands. He hadn't shaved in a while, and the stubble was a raspy purr against her palm. Dark smudges cradled his eyes. And all she wanted was to kiss away the bitterness from those proud features. "I forget how hard you've worked to get to this place."

He stiffened. "Do not pity me, Alessandra."

She smiled, her chest swimming with a most peculiar cocktail of emotions. "Antonio deserves my respect if nothing else. I'm sorry for speaking of him in such a manner. But—" she chose her words carefully "—he's determined to tether you to the past so tightly, V…" She pressed her mouth against his, desperate for a taste of him. Every word Antonio said to him, every meeting pulled Vincenzo away from the possibility of the future they could share. From finally releasing all the bitterness and anger he'd nursed for so long. From her. "And it terrifies the hell out of me."

That he didn't offer her words of reassurance made her belly swoop. Fear coated her skin with a cold chill and she started shivering.

There was change on the horizon—good and bad—so many chances that she could be split open and everything in her urged to run away again.

Instead, she embraced the fear and ache. She tightened her arms around him and let the vulnerability wash over her. Drown her. The lazy flick of his tongue against hers, the solid feel of him in her arms, the scent of him in her blood anchored her amidst her own fears. Rooted her.

Could the very man who might break her also give her strength to stay strong?

She'd have laughed at the question if it wasn't her heart in the balance.

His hands untangled hers from him. "You told Leonardo and Massimo about Antonio, about all the others."

"I didn't think it was a secret."

"I was a fool to believe that you would…" He moved away, his face set in tense lines, his mouth pinched.

As if she had truly betrayed him.

Suddenly, she felt as if she'd been given a painful insight into his thoughts.

Was that what Vincenzo expected of her? That she would betray him, abandon him at some point? That she would simply choose to walk away from all this?

But instead of feeling anger that he should trust her so little, Alex realized something else. This wasn't about his trust in her, this was about his own inability to trust. These were the scars left by a painful childhood where he hadn't had anyone to depend on. Anyone in his corner.

Her tone softened. "What Antonio wants for you is not healthy. So of course he'll paint this as some kind of deception on my part."

"I'm not discussing this with you."

"So don't," she said, suddenly angry herself. "We will add it to the list of things I'm not allowed to mention if I want to keep the delicate boat of our marriage from capsizing."

"What the hell are you talking about?"

"I'm not allowed to even ask you about your mother. I'm not allowed to be a part of Leo's and Massimo's lives, men I consider family. And I've made my peace with all that. To be with you.

"I did them one small favor in return for the hundreds they've bestowed on me. I'm tired of you constantly questioning my loyalty."

He sat down on the bed, his head in his hands, a deep sigh rolling out of him. He looked as though he had the weight of the world on his shoulders. And maybe he had carried it all this time. But things were different now. Changing.

And Alex was damned if she'd let him shoulder this alone anymore.

"Give me a chance to explain, V."

"Why did you tell them?"

"Because they deserved to know that their father's actions still had serious consequences, such far-reaching potential for destruction. Because I wanted to show you that you don't have to carry this burden alone. The burden of righting all the wrongs Silvio did, of bringing justice to those who can't fight for themselves."

He pulled her to him then, with a half-swallowed growl that sounded like a feral animal fighting for its last breath, and her heart thudded painfully in her breast. His face buried in her chest, his arms clung around her waist.

She sank her fingers into his crisp hair. "Leo's about to become a father to two children. Imagine you and I having a child and someone out there wishing our family so much ill will as these people do…" She shuddered and his arms tightened around her.

"How is it that you keep unraveling me?" he asked.

She looked down and their eyes held. Fused with a connection that they hadn't been able to deny from that first moment. The connection he wanted but not the force of emotion that strengthened it. The compromise and change it constantly asked of him, even the sacrifice it sometimes demanded.

"I've already decided not to demolish the villa," he said, and the small flicker of hope turned into a full-blown flame in her body. "But—"

She didn't want to hear any more. Pressing her finger to his mouth, she shimmied out of the flimsy robe and stood naked in front of him. Their kiss was a conflagration of desire and hope and such emotion that her heart stuttered in her chest.

His mouth was hard, rough; his kiss desperate, intense, a hard taking instead of giving. A demand for everything she could give.

She could sense it in the hunger in his eyes. In the tense jut of his muscles. But this wasn't pure lust. This was him reaching out to her when the ground was shifting beneath him. He palmed her breasts, pinched her nipples as she pulled his shirt out of his trousers with a fervent need. Tugged the zipper down and sneaked her hand inside.

His hips thrust against her hand as she molded the hard length of him. "I want to be inside you, now, *bella*."

"Yes, please," she whispered back. "Now."

Their mouths clung to each other as he shucked off the rest of his clothes.

A soft moan left her mouth as her body settled

against his—breast to chest, thigh to thigh, his abdominal muscles a hard slab of heat against hers. Wrapping her legs around him, she threw her head back and moaned.

And then he was inside her, her back against the wall, her front a delicious slide against all his muscles. But he didn't move inside her. Just held her like that, where she could feel him all over her body. His heart thudding against hers.

"We will live in that house, *bella*. You, me, our family. That's the only way I won't ruin it."

"But—"

"My wedding gift to you, *cara mia*. It's your choice now."

But he didn't wait for her answer. He started moving and her eyes rolled back.

Another searing kiss that swallowed not only her protest but her very breath. But she had no real protest anyway. She would take the little he gave her. He had changed for her. Because of her.

One corded arm rested near her head as he pulled out with a grunt and thrust back in. His teeth in the juncture of her neck kept that small edge to the waves of sensation building inside her, amplifying their sweetness in contrast.

With each upward jerk of his hips, she was pushed up and against the wall. With each wicked twist of his hips, sensation swelled and swirled downward. His face was savage in his utter lack of control. But even in the wake of such hunger, he didn't forget about her. Every upward thrust rubbed her in just the right place. When he tugged her nipple into his mouth, Alex fragmented. And he followed.

Alex held him as he released into her with a feral growl.

The words rose to her lips, desperate to be set free. The emotion in her chest taking the space of everything else. Rumbling like a volcano about to explode.

Instead, Alex buried her own teeth in the taut curve of his shoulder and swallowed away the words. Words never meant much to her anyway.

He'd shown her in actions that he cared about her. Which gave her hope. And hope was more than enough right now.

It was a long time later, tucked into the crook of his arm, his body a warm embrace, that Alex said, "What did Leo and Massimo do that angered Antonio so much? You never told me."

She'd expected him to shut her down; instead he only sighed. The darkness helped, she knew. And it wasn't just that. She'd seen something in him earlier. A shift. A change. A vulnerability that made her throat ache. And everything in her wanted to embrace that hope. Cling to it like she'd never done anything else before.

His fingers spread over her throat, his words a harsh whisper in the silence. "They offered financial reparation to the families of those that were cheated, crushed by their father. Training, jobs, even stock options in BFI."

Alex's heart lightened. Her trust in them was once again totally vindicated. She tempered her joy, sensing the tension in his powerful body. "But this is good, isn't it?"

"Is it? They're buying forgiveness, *cara*, don't you see?" But there was no heat in his tone. Resignation. Even acceptance maybe, she thought with more hope burgeoning inside her chest. "Which is why Antonio refused to even touch anything they offered."

"They don't need forgiveness. They didn't even need to redress Silvio's sins. But they've done it because they have a strong sense of right and wrong." She held his gaze in the darkness, saw the flicker of anger tamp down. He looked away, but Alex caught his expression before that. And suddenly she got it. "You're shocked that they're not the monsters you believed them to be for so long. That they're truly honorable men. Good men. It's not too late, V. If you just stretch your—"

"Not this again, Alessandra," he cut in harshly.

"Didn't this whole thing start as helping those who couldn't help themselves? To right the wrongs that Silvio Brunetti perpetrated? Or does it matter more that you have to be their savior than that they be saved at all?"

Vincenzo stilled, Alessandra's words piercing him like a thousand little cuts, stripping away the anger and bitterness he'd nursed for so many years. He wanted to yell at her to stop, to leave him be. To cease digging into him. Because if she stripped him bare of his need for revenge, his thirst for justice, if she took away this fight that had consumed his adult life, what would she find?

If he gave up his quest to take over BFI, what was left in him? Of him?

He'd meticulously planned and executed each and every move, and there was no way back from that. No way out from the hole he'd buried his heart in.

If he stopped now, how could he face the kind of man he'd become? How could he come back from that? How could he open himself up, make himself completely vulnerable at this late stage?

Because that anger, and bitterness, his ambition and his quest for revenge, he was fast realizing were his armor. Armor against hope and vulnerability.

Armor against the crippling knowledge that he had become a man who didn't deserve the woman lying next to him.

Armor against turning into a man who desperately needed love but didn't know how to give or receive it.

CHAPTER ELEVEN

ALEX STOOD IN front of the marble vanity a few days after they'd arrived back from New York and stared at her naked body in the steam fogged mirror. Something was different. Strange. She ran her fingers over her belly, and then up toward her breasts and cupped them. They felt achy and heavy, just as her entire body did.

Was all the stress of the past few months finally catching up with her? Or was it something else entirely?

No. It couldn't be. She had been on the pill the entire time—even before she'd met Vincenzo in Bali. After those first few nights together, after they'd been married, they'd stopped using condoms.

She wished she could talk to someone. But Greta was gone. As were the rest of them. All of them. This villa was their home now. Hers and Vincenzo's.

And it would be Charlie's, once they'd won custody of him.

And, she was suddenly quite sure, it would be this baby's too.

She kept her palm on her belly, waiting for panic to set in. For the mother of all freak-outs.

It didn't come.

Instead, total calm filled her. Even as she was aware that, right at this moment, Vincenzo and Leo and Massimo and Greta were all at the BFI towers in Milan for an emergency board meeting that Vincenzo had called.

He was almost there at the finish line, she knew.

There would be a vote of no confidence against Leo, and she also knew that Vincenzo had control of the majority. That he would be voted CEO of Brunetti Finances Inc. any minute now.

For all that she hated to see Greta and Leo and Massimo leave this villa, this war Vincenzo had waged for so long would finally be done with now. And they didn't hate her, or him.

Vincenzo would have achieved his goal. He would be finished. And their life could begin. Once they were a family, once he had everything he wanted—Charlie and her and this baby, maybe he would even finally open himself up to understanding what the Brunettis meant to her.

If Leo and Massimo could let his actions go, couldn't Vincenzo be convinced to let the past go? If he could do that, he would be free. His heart would be free.

Alex smiled at her reflection. Anything was possible. And that hope was a powerful thing inside her.

Vincenzo went in search of his wife upstairs in the villa, a sense of inexplicable dread descending on him.

All of Milan's financial society was downstairs and out in the gardens, celebrating his victory. Lauding him. Courting his favor. Already catering to him.

He had soundly defeated Leonardo at the vote of no confidence. But of course, he would have enjoyed it so much more if Alex hadn't disappeared after barely showing her face. Both when he'd returned from the board meeting earlier and tonight at the party.

Any irritation he felt died down as he walked into the terrace and found her looking out at the garden and the lake. The magnificent view did nothing to dim her beauty.

She turned and he drank her in. The soft pink evening gown draped over her curves, highlighting the lithe body. Her beautiful hair flew in the breeze, the diamond choker he'd bought her yesterday glittering at her neck.

And yet, one look at her pinched face told him that for all her standing by him as the perfect wife, she was less than happy.

No, she was miserable.

But it wasn't just physical exhaustion. The vitality that had struck him like lightning on their first meeting, the joy he'd seen on the day of their impromptu wedding was nowhere to be seen.

Guilt nagged at him like a persistently sharp shard of glass stuck in his skin. He hated having to admit that he was responsible for that haunted look in her eyes. For the first time in his life, he had an emotional obligation to another person and he was fast failing in keeping it.

"Are you happy now?" she asked.

He shrugged, wary of the bite to her tone. "Alessandra, I want to celebrate tonight. I want to take you to bed, *bella*. Not have a down-and-dirty fight. Not again."

She nodded, and it was as if there was a brittle wall around her. "I wanted to celebrate your victory with you tonight too. I even thought of it as freedom, you know. Freedom from the shackles you've bound yourself with. Freedom from the past.

"So that you could be mine. Only mine."

"I am yours, *bella*. I've told you that before."

"Only under your conditions, V. I see that now. And still, I was happy. For you. I wanted to go to bed with you, to be held by you while I told you the most glorious news that I've been dying to share all day. I wanted to…" A silent tear rolled down her cheek. "I wanted so much. Everything. It was all in my grasp."

He walked to her, that sense of dread building inside his chest, choking off his breath. "Alessandra, you knew this was going to happen, *bella*."

"I knew it. I begged Leo and Massimo to forgive you. I told them about your mother, about how much you've been through. I made my peace with the fact that you're who you are and that despite it all I… I loved you. So much, V. I love you more than anything else in the world. And that's why this hurts so much." She rubbed a hand over her chest and gasped for a breath. "It feels like my heart is breaking all over again."

Her words were like punches coming at him, stealing his breath. She loved him. *Cristo*, she loved him. It rang through his body like a peal of painful truth. Like the ground was shifting beneath him and he didn't know what to grasp for an anchor.

"Alessandra—"

She jerked away from him. "I always thought I would be able to save Leo and Massimo and Greta from you. I thought… But they didn't need saving. Even after you took the CEO position from Leonardo, even after you took this house, their home from them, they're fine. You're the one who's lost everything that matters. You're the one who needs saving."

He felt as if she'd slapped him. "I don't need saving."

She went on, as if he hadn't spoken. "But that's

the most important thing I've learned in the last few months.

"No one else can save us, can they? However much I want to, I can't save you. From yourself of all things. We have to do it ourselves. We have to want to be saved. The only hope is that someone we love, who loves us, will stand by us while we do it.

"Someone who believes in us even when we don't. When we're so blinded by fear that…we can't see a way forward."

She clasped his cheek, tears pouring down her own. "You did that for me. You made me realize I should stay and fight. You made me…" She buried her face in his throat, and her tears drenched him. Seared his bare skin. The weight of her love for him burned him.

He wanted to pull her close and hold her. But he couldn't. Not when he himself felt as if he were drowning. "Alessandra, just tell me what's happened. Tell me—"

"You know, you were right when you said I didn't understand the magnitude of the consequences Greta wreaked on you that day. I didn't truly comprehend the depth of pain you must have felt every time you saw her. To have all this and not even be able to tell your mother that…"

"Alessandra! You knew all this when you made your choice, *bella*. What has changed?"

She tilted her head up, her gaze crystal clear.

Her palm went to her belly and she held it there. "Discovering that I'm pregnant."

Another punch. Another blinding hit. Vincenzo couldn't speak for several seconds. His gaze went to her hand on her belly and to her eyes that glowed with conviction. "You're... pregnant?" He pushed his hand through his hair. "When—"

"Yeah. Can you believe it? I was all set to freak out. But when I saw the test come back positive... I was actually giddy. You and I created this life. I thought this was the universe's way of giving me what I wanted. A family. A child to love created with the man I adore. I had everything I wanted."

"Alex, if this is good news, why are you crying?"

"I was overjoyed. I decided magnanimously that I would forgive Greta for what she'd done to you. I...called her. I could tell something was seriously wrong and I made her tell me how you threatened her and that my happiness was the price she had to pay. Her love for me and my love for you was your currency. Do you even realize how wrong that is? Do you—?"

"Alessandra, listen to me. Today's win at BFI—"

"No! I've listened to you enough. I can't do it anymore, V. You know why?" She wiped her cheeks angrily. "Because the last shred of hope I had that we could salvage this marriage is gone.

Whatever you say now, you can't bring it back." Fury shone in her beautiful eyes, radiated from her body.

"You promised me you'd never use me against them. You said you'd keep me out of this infernal war you've been waging and you broke your word. You used Leo's and Massimo's guilt for what other people did to you to drive them out of here.

"You think love is a weakness to be exploited... You will never be released from this poison. You will never open yourself to love. It's too late. The poison has already festered inside you for far too long.

"And while that might have been okay for me, it's not okay for this child. It's not okay for Charlie."

"So you're giving up on us again?"

"No, I'm refusing to accept anything less than what I deserve. I deserve to be with a man who will at least acknowledge that love is important. This child and Charlie deserve to grow up with a father who has the capacity to love them."

He reared back, stung. "I will love our child."

"Will you? Will you tell him or her about what you did to your brothers? Will you speak about the cousins it has? What is the legacy you're creating for this child, V? One of love or one of hatred and revenge?"

"Don't do this, Alessandra," he said, and a

part of Alex melted at the desperation she heard in his voice.

She was the one breaking apart and he looked equally ravaged. "So you're ready to destroy everything you wanted? You're giving up on Charlie too?"

"No, I'm not. I will never give up on Charlie. And I will gain custody of him because you will help me do that, V. This relationship is over between us but not in the eyes of the world. Not until I have Charlie, safe with me. You owe me this. I'm hoping you have enough honor left in your body to see that promise through at least.

"As for raising him alone, I do have a family. Leo and Massimo will support me if I need help. Charlie already has a family that will love him, through me."

"And this child? Our child?"

"I will love our child too. Fiercely. You made me see that.

"I will take on anyone and anything in the world to protect our baby. Including you. But then, you're not the kind of man that would separate a mother from her child, are you? I won't lose sleep over that worry, at least."

"You're walking out on me and yet you still have such faith in me, *bella*?"

"I do. Because you're only punishing yourself, V. I see you watch Leo and Massimo with such an ache in your eyes. You can't understand the depth of Greta's love for me. Your support network for close to two decades has been people who were invested in seeing you destroy the Brunettis. \

"You have made an island of yourself.

"But I can't bear to see you in pain. I can't bear to see the loneliness in your eyes, the need for connection. I refuse to stand here and watch it eat away at you, month after month, year after year. I refuse to let the corrosive shadow of your grief and guilt consume me and two more innocent lives.

"You wanted this empire, V. Well, you got it. But you haven't got me."

Anger raged in his eyes, and a stillness came over him. "At least don't lie to me that you love me, *bella.*"

"I do love you. With all my heart. I truly understand what it means to love someone so much that all you want is their happiness. Their well-being. But it's not a weakness, V. Despite all the pain in my heart, I can't call it that."

And with that, she walked away from him, head held high. Out of his life.

Leaving him standing empty-handed on the grounds of the very empire he'd built.

Alessandra's words haunted Vincenzo as he walked around the hallowed halls of his ancestors, with a bottle of Leonardo's fine Scotch hanging from his fingers.

For the first time in his life he was filthy drunk, his self-control shot to hell. Apparently, there were a lot of those happening currently—these first times in his life.

He walked from room to room—he couldn't bear to be in the bedroom he had shared with her for more than a few minutes. He walked from the vast kitchen that had rung with laughter only last week when Natalie's younger brother had visited and Neha had screamed that the babies were playing soccer in her belly to the conservatory, where every piece of silk reminded him of his wife's skin; to the lounge that housed the ancient piano; to the arched hallway with portraits of his ancestors hanging there, looking down upon him with, it seemed, approval.

All my life, our father constantly told me that I wasn't good enough to belong with them. That I would never be good enough. But then it took Natalie to make me see that it was okay to not belong with those monsters.

Massimo had told him that during one of their midnight chats weeks ago, those long nights where more than once he'd found himself wandering the villa and run into his younger brother doing the same thing.

Just thinking of the brilliant tech genius as his younger brother, as the man who had Natalie's hard-won loyalty and love, sat like a boulder in Vincenzo's throat, jammed in there to force him to acknowledge the connection, the affection he had developed for the irreverent genius, despite himself.

What did it say that when Vincenzo looked at those same faces of Brunetti ancestors, he saw their approval? Was he truly Silvio Brunetti's legacy then—a legacy of cruelty and hatred and destruction?

He had hated this family for so long. He had used that hatred to propel himself to incredible heights. He'd thought there would be victory once he had achieved his ambition, his revenge.

Suddenly, the consuming force of his life was gone and he felt as empty as this damned house.

He even walked to the state-of-the-art tech lab that had belonged to Massimo. The underground lab that had once been a wine cellar, Alessandra had told him with a twinkle in her eyes.

She'd been happy here and he had taken it away.

He punched in the entry password and walked around the now-empty lab. Then he made the trek to the greenhouse that Leonardo had renovated for himself.

The greenhouse, he'd learned, had once belonged to Leonardo's mother. Silvio Brunetti's first wife—a woman who had run away in the dark of the night, leaving her five-year-old son with the monster, the very monster she had run from.

The damp air inside the greenhouse was a warm blast against his chilled skin as he walked around, touching the parts here and there, imagining Leonardo and his very pregnant wife, Neha, in here, making plans for their children.

And now because of him, this was empty too.

Leonardo had given up ownership of this house, a real estate asset, two centuries of legacy that should have gone to his children, to Vincenzo far too easily.

He slammed the door of the greenhouse behind him and walked up the pathway back to the house. He had no idea how many times he'd made that trip recently—a sort of pilgrimage from the villa to the laboratory to the greenhouse to the conservatory, and then back around again.

Everywhere he looked he saw Alessandra laughing, crying, kissing him, teasing Massimo, hugging Leonardo.

He felt like a forlorn ghost, a cursed specter, haunting these halls, the very hallowed halls he had once wanted to belong to. He had everything he had ever wanted.

And yet he had lost the one thing he desperately needed. The one thing he couldn't live without—Alessandra's love, her laughter, her smiles, her kisses, her tears, her joyful presence.

He hated admitting it, but there it was.

All his life he had been alone, so he shouldn't have minded this so much. But this loneliness was different. This was deeper, harder, felt in a place he hadn't known existed within him. Felt by a different man. A man who should've stopped long ago, but hadn't because then he'd have had to face what he'd become. How empty he was inside.

And he stood in that place of emptiness now anyway.

The sound of footsteps had him prowling into the lounge, his heart thudding so hard in his chest that its beat roared in his ears. Hope oozed out of his every pore, coating him with a layer of desperation so thick and rabid that he couldn't shake it off. It was unlike anything he'd ever felt, almost felling him to his knees.

The moon outside painted two dark silhouettes through the open archway. He blinked as the crystal chandelier overhead burst into life, throwing dazzlingly painful light over the room. The black-and-white-checkered marble swam in front of his eyes, and he instinctively reached for the grand piano to steady himself.

He looked up then and cursed out loud.

Massimo burst out laughing. Leonardo remained serious, but there was a twitch to his mouth that Vincenzo wanted to rip off with his bare hands.

"What the hell do you two want?" he demanded, straightening.

"We came to check on you," Massimo said. He took in Vincenzo's disheveled state with a distinctly obvious grin. "I have to admit, Leo. I'd hoped to find him like this. This almost makes up for everything he did to us. Almost."

Vincenzo let out another curse. "Get out! Get out of my house!"

Leonardo reached him, a sneer curling his mouth into a twist. And finally, Vincenzo could no longer deny the resemblance between himself and this man... This man who he had no doubt now would have made a spectacular older brother. A role model. A protector. "My wife is about to give birth any moment! To twins, you ungrateful bastard! And here I am in the middle of the night, checking up on you because she asked us to."

Massimo laughed again, and both he and Leo cursed him soundly. "Our older brother, as you can tell, is quite nervous. Everything is out of his control with Neha and the babies and it's driving him crazy. And he's driving her crazy." Leo growled. "Which is why she begged me to take him on this midnight run," Massimo finished. "I left Natalie behind because if she's here, she won't let Leo beat some sense into you."

Vincenzo rubbed his head, trying to figure out the puzzle of what they meant, who they were talking about. Even the threat of Leo's fists couldn't distract him from trying to figure it out. "Wait, who asked you to check up on me? You're not talking about Neha, are you?"

"Your bloody wife, who else?" Leo roared. "The woman whose heart you so thoroughly broke. The woman you don't deserve."

"She walked out on me," Vincenzo offered in a lame, pathetic voice. "And you're right. I don't deserve her. Still she gave me a chance to re-deem myself. And I destroyed that chance. I... drove her away. I...killed whatever she felt for me with my own hands."

Whatever he'd been about to say died on Mas-simo's shocked lips.

His knees finally gave out, and Vincenzo slid to the floor. He buried his head in his hands. *Cristo*, what had he done? What was this cursed villa, the blasted company, even this world, to him, without her? He looked up, fear unlike any-thing he'd ever known clamping his belly tight. "I... I won everything and lost everything all in one fell swoop."

Both men knelt on either side of him. And he felt shame and vulnerability and something else lodge in his throat, cutting off his breath. "Why are you here after I drove you out of your own home?"

"We can't imagine what you've endured for so long. What it feels like to see your mother and not have her see you in return. But actions can be rectified, V," Massimo said kindly, using the abbreviation only *she* used for him. "You can still prove that Alex's faith in you was not misplaced."

"And because we've each been here," Leo added. "In this place of destruction. Standing on a pile of ashes that we created with our own actions. Not our father's actions, Vincenzo." It was the first time Leo had said his name. "Not Greta's. Ours. You're the one who's letting the woman who loves you go."

Vincenzo pushed himself off the floor.

"Go to her, but only if you think you can do right by her. Only if…" Leo's tone edged into that warning zone again.

"Alex deserves the best a man can give," Vincenzo added, and both men nodded.

"We have to want to be saved. The only hope is that someone we love, who loves us, will stand by us while we do it."

She'd been right. So right. Vincenzo hoped with every cell in him that she would still stand by him. That he was worthy of that.

"Now, I would suggest a grand gesture of some sort," Massimo added, clapping him on the back.

Vincenzo rubbed his eyes and stared at the two men whose forgiveness he still needed to beg. But not yet. Not now. "*Cristo*, if this is the kind of psychobabble that Alessandra thinks I miss out on by not being one of you, then I shall gladly tell her how wrong she is. I…don't need a couple of Brunetti bastards to tell me I messed up. Royally."

"Ha! We came to tell you that you chose a woman who will forgive you almost anything. If you grovel hard enough, V."

Leo stood up. "Massimo has enough experience with that if you want some guidance."

Vincenzo looked at them. "This is not easy for me. I've never asked anyone for anything in my entire life. I have never—" He stopped and swallowed. "Whatever I have to say, she deserves to hear it first."

CHAPTER TWELVE

IT WAS PANIC.

It was sheer, unadulterated panic that sat like a boulder in his chest, that crawled up his throat like nausea at regular intervals, which had made him lose his head. Which had made him chase her halfway around the world—the wrong way.

Of course, she hadn't been in New York. Nor in Milan. Nor in Beijing sourcing fabric.

She was at the place where it had all started. Where, by some stroke of fate, he'd tangled with the woman who would end up becoming his saving grace.

The lush greenery surrounding the small village of Ubud hit Vincenzo with an onslaught of memories as he walked through the villa they had stayed in the last time to the private beach area behind it.

He found her sitting on the massive deck, a glass of water on the table next to her and a paperback on her stomach.

She was sleeping. But not peacefully. Even

from the length of the deck, he could see her eye-lids fluttering. Her body tensing up.

Guilt raked its fingers through him.

He made his way to her softly, loath to disturb her rest. He was about to sit down when she startled awake.

Her golden-brown eyes found him, only half-awake.

"Hello, Princess."

"V…?"

She rubbed her eyes, an innocent action that made his chest ache. When she realized he wasn't a figment of her imagination, she sat up. And her mouth took on the stiff slant he hated.

"You ran away again, *bella*," he said, finding that his voice was scratchy. As if he hadn't used it in months.

"But I told you I was leaving this time," she said in a low voice. Her chin lifted. "What are you doing here, V? I already told you the hearing for Charlie's custody is in New York in two weeks."

"I thought I would accompany you there."

"I appreciate the consideration but I don't need it." The silence bore down upon them. He saw her swallow, as if she was bracing herself. "This polite courtesy needn't be extended when it's just the two of us. Hopefully, it will all be over soon. I'll get custody of Charlie and we don't need to see each other again."

"*Cristo*, Alex! Don't talk to me as if I'm a stranger."

"I'm not. I just… I need to be strong. I can't keep seeing you and stay sane."

He nodded, that strange fear swallowing away the one thing he needed to say. Instead he said, "How are you feeling?"

"Good. I… I have morning sickness, except it's all the time. Like morning, noon and night. I…but apparently, it's normal. For some people."

"Alessandra—"

"But I'm lonely, you know." She rubbed her chest as if she could dislodge that ache. "I miss Greta and Leo and Massimo. And Natalie. And Neha and the babies. Did you know she had the babies?"

"*Si,*" he said, smiling despite the pain in his throat. "They are…healthy and thriving. They are naming them Maya and Matteo. The girl child is especially beautiful, just like her mother—"

"Wait, you went to see them?"

"*Si.* I… I asked Leo if I could and he said yes."

Her eyes widened. "Oh." She looked away, but not before he saw the flash of hope. But when she looked back at him, her eyes were full of a wariness that was like a knife to his chest. "Why?"

He considered answers and discarded them, incredibly nervous for the first time in his life. "I went because I… I knew you would appreciate hearing firsthand how they're doing. But

I also went—" he swallowed "—because that bastard Massimo told me he was going to be the fun uncle they adored and I couldn't have that." The words kept coming like a torrent, unchecked. Unabashed. "But then I also thought of what you said. How they're my niece and nephew and how they'd be our child's cousins and I realized that I wanted all that for our child.

"I don't want our child to grow up all alone. Like I did.

"I want him or her to be part of a big family. A clan. A dynasty."

Tears poured out of his beautiful wife's eyes. A sound, like the combination of a sob and a moan, came hurtling out of her mouth. Vincenzo went to his knees in front of her. And buried his face in her belly. "*Ti amo*, Alessandra. With all my heart. Without you, there's nothing in my world, *cara*."

"V, if this is a game again—"

"It is not, *bella*. I don't think it ever was a game to me. You felled me from the first moment I met you, Princess. I just didn't realize exactly what that meant to me all this time."

He raised his head, his breath suspended at the love he saw blazing in her eyes. It was almost unbearable, the strength and depth of emotion she clearly felt for him. It shook him to his core that there might come a day when she wouldn't look at him like that. That she might leave again, another day.

But he couldn't think like that. He couldn't doubt her love or his. He couldn't keep looking at his past actions and ruin his future.

"If I tell you something, will you believe me?"

She nodded warily.

"I never used Greta's vote against Leo at the last board meeting." He pressed his palm against her mouth. "I know that that's not much solace. I'd already threatened to use her love for you, your happiness against them, and that itself was unforgivable.

"But that same day, I also talked to Antonio, and something he said made me realize it was he who leaked my relationship to the Brunettis to the press all those months ago. He made a calculated risk that I would be able to recover any lost ground, but his primary goal was for me to leave you and carry on with my plans for vengeance, regardless of how much it would hurt me.

"And I realized how much hatred he has in him. In him, I saw my future, *bella*, the companionship of loneliness and hatred instead of family and love. I had already begun questioning everything I had done against my own brothers.

"But to turn away from my path completely, it terrified me. It meant I had to face what sort of a man I had become. It meant…facing the fact that I'm not worthy of you."

"But I never wanted some perfect man, V. I

wanted you. I loved you despite everything you'd done."

"Forgive me, *bella*, for not seeing that before. Do you know, I wake up in the middle of the night with the most horrible nightmare now?"

She frowned. "What do you dream of?"

"That I didn't follow you here that first time. That for some reason or the other, I changed my mind about coming to Bali. That I never met you until I had already ruined everything. My own future with both my hands. That I never got the chance for you to love me.

"And I wake up, thrashing, the sheets cold around me. My chest the coldest of all.

"I reach for you and you're not there.

"You saved me, *bella*. From myself.

"And I will love you all my life for it."

She was sobbing again, as if her heart was breaking, and Vincenzo folded her into his arms. He settled into the lounger with her in his lap, crooning to her, kissing her temple. Rocking her. Cursing himself for causing her this much pain.

"Every night I went to bed, hoping that you'd come the next day. Walking away from you was like ripping out my own heart and I couldn't do it again, V."

"Shh...*tesoro*. You will never have to leave me again. Never, bella. Never will I doubt your love for me. Never will I make you doubt mine for you."

She kissed him, and Vincenzo felt as if he was born again. He became a different man in her kiss, in her embrace. "When you're ready, we will fly to New York and see Charlie. And then we'll take him back to the villa, to meet the rest of our family."

"Really?" she said, looking at him like he was a hero.

And for the first time in his life, Vincenzo felt as if he was, if not exactly a hero, at least not a villain.

"I have tried to return the villa to Leo and Massimo. In fact, I begged them to take it back, to come back home, and I think Massimo in particular enjoyed it. He kept urging Leo to torment me a little more, and Natalie kept yelling at him to leave me alone.

"After all these years, she still has faith in me. She threw herself behind me without a moment's thought." He looked away.

Fingers in his hair, Alex tugged his head back around until he looked into her eyes. "Because she loves you, V. Don't you get it? She's already seen you at your worst and she still loves you. That kind of love…it doesn't go away overnight."

He kissed her deep and hard. "I'm finally beginning to understand that, Princess."

"What happened then?"

"Leonardo won't take it back. He's having another villa built to his own design and he wants to live there with Neha and the babies and her mother. And Massimo and Natalie said the Brunetti villa is too big for them."

"What about BFI?"

He swallowed, shame filling up his throat. "Leo...doesn't want the CEO chair back either. He said that he's carried the mantle of the Brunetti legacy, of BFI's weight, for too many years. He'll still work for the company, with me, but not as the CEO. I asked Massimo if he wanted it, and he backed away as if it was the very devil. He said he was happier running BCS, that the bureaucratic nonsense wasn't for him and keeping the jackals on the board happy should be punishment enough for me."

"Are you okay with that?" she asked him perceptively.

Vincenzo shrugged. "Only if you are, *bella*. I never want you to think that BFI or the villa or anything else is more important to me than you are."

"I won't, V. I never thought you were power hungry even before, and I don't now."

"So the villa is ours, but only if you want it. Only if you'll be happy living there."

"And Greta? Can I ask her to live with us, V?"

"Is this another test, *bella*? Have I crushed your faith in me so badly?"

She cupped his cheek. "No, not at all. You know when I pushed her to tell me what you'd threatened to do, she…she broke down into tears. She…said she'd hated having to tell me what you did. She said, for all the wrongs you'd done me, she was sure you did love me. In your own Brunetti way, she added. As if that pigheaded stubbornness was something to be proud of."

He smiled as Alex pulled him close and kissed him. "You both need time to heal, V. And it's a damn big villa. We can even have your mother and her nurses live with us. In fact, I insist on it."

Vincenzo swallowed the tears that clogged his throat and looked into the eyes of the woman who'd given him everything. "It's not always easy to have her around."

She shrugged. "But family is never easy, right? I have always wanted a big family, and you and me and Charlie and this baby and Greta and your mother…this is our big family, V. This is everything I always wanted."

"You're my heart and soul, Princess, and my happiness lies wherever you are. With this baby. With Charlie. So, yes to everything, *bella*. To a life full of laughter and joy."

"Yes, please," she whispered against his mouth, and he felt as if his heart would burst out of his chest. For there was a strange giddy quality to it he had never known before. Love.

EPILOGUE

Eight months later

ALEX PRESSED HERSELF back with a deep moan as strong hands descended on her hips. As rock-hard thighs cradled hers. As the hardness she ached for nestled enticingly into her buttocks.

Vincenzo nuzzled into her neck, and she happily threw her head back, more than greedy for her husband's caresses after a busy three months.

"I've missed you, Princess," he murmured, his lips and teeth and tongue wreaking havoc on the sensitive spot on her neck, sending live wires of sensation straight to her sex.

"I've missed you too," Alex whispered, pressing her fingers onto his. And then pulling them up until his hands cradled her breasts. He immediately obliged, rolling her already tightening nipples into harder peaks with his clever fingers.

"Think we have a few minutes before we have to rescue Greta from down there?"

Alex looked down at the front lawn, where

Charlie was running around in circles, Vincenzo's mother kept darting looks at the little baby boy in the stroller, calling him Vincenzo, and Greta was very efficiently keeping an eye on the whole lot of them. "Greta doesn't need to be rescued at all. She soothes your fractious son, Luca, and your mother all at the same time with one magic word uttered in that commanding voice of hers. They both respond to her so well, V. It's really something to watch."

He didn't say it, but Alex felt the slight tension in his body when his mother ventured closer to their son's stroller. And his exhale of relief when she simply bent to pick up the pacifier their son had spat out and plonked it back into his mouth with a tenderness that made Alex's throat ache.

She turned around, determined to distract him. The kiss she took from him—a heated tangle of teeth and tongues—was nowhere near enough. The last eight months had been laughter and joy and pain and sometimes plain awkwardness as her reticent husband learned to embrace all the things that came with being part of a large family.

But not a day went by when he didn't let her know how much he loved her. Not a day went by when he didn't show how much their sons, Luca and Charlie, and Leo and Massimo meant to him.

How wrong she'd been to think him a frog. No, her husband was indeed a prince among men.

For he had learned how to love when he'd never really known it for most of his life.

Keeping her arms around his neck, she kissed his jaw. "You don't have to worry about her, V. Greta and I took alternating turns watching her, not forgetting her nurse is always there too."

He nodded, his brow relaxing. "I just…it's a habit, that's all, *bella*."

"I know," Alex said, rubbing her nose against his. "How did your lunch with Antonio go? Is he coming around yet?"

Vincenzo shrugged. "I don't know. But I will not just abandon him, in spite of what he did."

"Of course you won't. Maybe you should invite him to lunch here next time. Don't you think he should meet the little monster that is your son?"

"Ah…so he's my son when he's a monster and yours when he sleeps like an angel?" Amazement spiraled through Vincenzo. He knew that Antonio's intensity still made Alex a bit wary. But she was willing to try again for his sake. "You won't mind?"

"He's a part of your life, V. He was there for you before me. And like you said, he's an old man, settled in his bitterness. We can't expect him to come around just like that."

Vincenzo took her mouth in a hard kiss that still left him hungry. "*Ti amo, bella.* More and more every day." When he reached for the zipper on her dress, she slipped out of his embrace.

"I need you, Princess. Desperately," he said, unbuttoning his shirt.

"But we have only a few minutes before Leo and Neha and the babies and Massimo and Natalie descend upon us."

He caught her and stole another kiss. "I'm sure I can satisfy you in a few minutes, *bella*."

Alex shook her head, all the while running her greedy palms over his hard, lean chest. "Ah…but I don't want quick satisfaction. I want a whole night of indulgence, V. I want…everything tonight."

Vincenzo groaned but nodded, anticipation building inside of him already. When she'd have run away, he caught her, lifted her in his arms and brought her to the chaise that looked over the window and settled on it with her in her arms.

"Then let me just hold you, *bella*. Before the boys or my mother or your stepmother or someone else demands your attention. Just let me have you for myself, *si*?"

She nodded and burrowed into him and only then did his heartbeat settle into a steady pace.

And Vincenzo sat there like that, with the woman he adored more and more each day, in his arms, his life sweeter and richer than anything he could have ever imagined.

* * * * *

Adored The Flaw in His Marriage Plan
by Tara Pammi?
You're sure to enjoy the first two instalments in
The Scandalous Brunetti Brothers miniseries:
An Innocent to Tame the Italian
and
A Deal to Carry the Italian's Heir
Available now!

And why not explore these other
Tara Pammi stories?

Bought with the Italian's Ring
Blackmailed by the Greek's Vows
Sheikh's Baby of Revenge
Sicilian's Bride for a Price

All available now!